SUNSET RAIN

a collection of short stories

300 SOUTH MEDIA GROUP

NEW YORK

This book is presented as a collection.

ISBN-13: 978-0-9970356-4-3

First Printing May 2021

Cover & Interior Design by 300 South Media Group

300SMG.com

DEDICATION

To all the storytellers, the dreamers, and those who hold our imagination through these words. Thank you

To all the readers who escape through these pages, without you, these words are just ink stains with no meaning.

TABLE OF CONTENTS

On behalf of the writers, authors, and 300 South Media Group, I'd like to thank you for your interest in Sunset Rain, for reading the stories shared on these pages, and for giving a voice to the words.

Jay Long

For more information on each contributing author, please refer to the ABOUT THE AUTHORS section at the end of the book.

We also ask you to follow 300 South Media Group on Facebook, where new authors and all upcoming projects will be featured.

FACEBOOK.COM/300SOUTHPUBLISHING

ALSO AVAILABLE FROM 300 SOUTH MEDIA GROUP

Rise From Within (various authors)
Eternal Echoes (Jay Long)
Timeless Chatter Between the Heart and Mind (Jay Long)

INTRODUCTION

When submissions for Sunset Rain were opened, I had no idea what to expect. There were no restrictions on the genre or subject matter of the pieces to be considered for inclusion. I soon found great pleasure in reading some great stories.

21 writers from around the world contributed to this project. Their words were not censored, the text was left the way they wrote it--the way it was intended--including different regional spellings for common words.

Sunset Rain is a collection of creative non-fiction, and fictional short stories. Within these pages, writers have created stories covering multiple genres and styles--all with a plot twist.

It is important to note, the stories within may contain subjects that are disturbing to some.

I couldn't be more proud of all those who made this book possible. Each story is fueled by creativity. I am so happy to share with you these words--these stories and hope you enjoy them as much as I did putting them together

Jay Long

300 South Media Group

A MOMENT IN TIME

by Wil R.P. McCarthy

"You can't do this Eric!" Said an old man in a lab coat.

The middle-aged man who was getting into a capsule responded in a calm tone. "Listen, Walter, I am going to do this. I will save her. I know I can."

Walter wrung his hands and smoothed his coat, "But Eric, we don't know what this will do to the timeline! What it may do to you! To all of us!"

Eric looked at the kindly old man who had been his mentor for half a lifetime and said, "I don't care! I have to save her." The argument settled in his mind Eric closed the door to the chamber. The machine which had been pre-programmed began the countdown after he strapped himself in.

The mechanized voice counted, "Ten... nine... eight..." Walter pounded on the door but inside he could not hear what he was yelling. "Seven... six... five...," the computer continued. He saw Walter back away from the time capsule but he knew he had made the countdown irreversible. "Four... three... two... one... initialize." The capsule filled with light and he could not see. Everything was white, everything was...

He found himself standing in a clearing and next to him was a small bag. He raised his hands and looked at them with wonder. Gone were the lines of age, and they were smaller. He had jumped into his younger self as planned. He looked around and recognized where he was. He was a couple of miles from her house. This is where they used to come to play.

He looked into the bag, "Yes, it worked," he said. Inside were his supplies, he took his chronometer out. He had designed this one to adjust automatically, he hoped, to the time fluctuation. Studying it, he sighed in relief. It worked. He was back. He just needed to find her before his hour ran out.

He grabbed the bag and set off towards her house. As he walked through the woods of his youth, he was struck by the memories of it all. He had not come back here in decades. He was lost in his revelry, his mind wondering on the phantoms of the past. Realizing this, he snapped himself out of it and looked at his meter. He only had thirty minutes left. Pocketing it he increased his pace with renewed fervor.

As he approached the fence to her yard, he saw he only had ten minutes before the auto-recall initiated. He heard the yelling then. Her father was drunk again. Pulling the pistol from the bag he quietly swore to himself he would not let this happen again. He dropped his bag and ran towards the house.

He heard the smashing of plates against the walls and he knew he did not have much time. Kicking the door that was always unlocked open he burst into the house gun at the ready. He saw her cowering before her father. The drunk bastard had a baseball bat raised above her ready to swing.

"No!" Eric yelled and pulled the trigger repeatedly. Shot after shot rang out until the chamber emptied and all that was left was the clicking of an empty mag. Red spots started to form on

her father's white tee, and he slumped over falling to the ground where he laid not moving.

In the silence afterward, she softly said, "Why... why would you do that?" There were tears in her eyes, "Dad... daddy... daddy...," she held onto the form of her dead father and cried.

Eric said, "I had to, he was going to kill you."

She looked up at him, tears streaking down her face, "I'll never forgive you!" she exclaimed.

In his pocket, his meter started to beep, "No," he said, "Not now, I need more time."

Everything around him started to turn white. It enveloped him and the last thing he heard was her say, "I'll make you pay for this." All went white...

He found himself in absolute darkness. Confused, he went to stand up and banged his head on a very low ceiling. Panic filled him. Reaching out he realized he was in a confined cubic room. He started to shout, "What's going on... Walter... Walter let me out!" he continued this for minutes, calling out in fear.

Finally, he heard footsteps and a small panel opened in one of the walls. A gruff voice said, "Shut up, or I'll have the warden extend your time in solitary for a full month."

"Solitary?" Eric questioned, "I'm in prison?"

The voice behind the opening laughed, "No you're in a spa. Come on. Has the confinement made you loony? You've been serving a life sentence for thirty years now. Now shut the fuck up or else." The small opening of light shut and he was once again left in total darkness. He realized he had saved her but he had lost everything else. And in the dark of his cell, he began to cry.

THE EXCHANGE

by Jamie Santomasso

He lay still as if slumbering peacefully in dreamland. His body had not moved since the night before, but this was typical as he was a sound sleeper. Her voice drifted in from the hall; his daily alarm clock to wake in the morning. He did not rise. She called again; her voice laced with playful laughter, she often knew him to dream as soundly as the dead.

Her voice yielded no results, so she entered the bedroom to pry him from the blankets. Upon entering she took in the horrific scene. Her lover lay on the bed, knife clutched in his fist. His chest bled red. The gravity of what she was looking at sinking in: the blade was the enforcer, his heart the victim, his life the casualty.

She knelt on the bed before her motionless lover, covering him with her body as despair flooded her and her heart shattered into pieces. She sobbed into his chest, clutching his lifeless, crimson-stained hand. Where there once was life, only coldness remained. Her lament overwhelming, she screamed to the heavens in gasping anguish: "Return my love to me, or if not let me follow his path so that we may be together! Let my betrothed live, and I shall take his place! "

She cried until the tears could flow no longer. They had been taken from her, just as her beloved had fallen. She cursed the sky and the God who reigned above. She wished a thousand times over to be able to hold him once more, begging to join him in his eternal resting place.

But she could not follow, for he had been taken by mortal sin and crossed the waters Styx, having paid Hades his penance of copper coins. He now lay in the Seventh Circle to endure his fate, a place where her pureness could not enter. She had been forbidden... her passage denied.

As she mourned on the bed the Star of Venus shined its celestial light down on her, illuminating the room around her. Phosphoros emerged from the shadows of the corner, approached the girl and her ill-fated lover. His emerald eyes surveyed the scene. He smelled of calming lilac and wore a knowing smile. His black cape adorning him like a majestic robe. He approached with care and caution, observing the sadness overflowing from her. He held took her hand as to offer heartfelt condolence.

"I can feel your tears, little one. They tear at my heart like marionette strings. No one should experience such pain. Let me cure you of the despair that has taken you," his soothing tone spoke.

"My love has left my side. Death has taken him, and I will give the heavens to have him back," she said through tear-stained sobs.

"The heavens are not yours to give, my beauty. But I can give you your lover back and you may live a millennia in bliss." He took the girl's hand and she stood, observing his beautiful face with skeptical eyes.

"All you need do is give me a gift of my choosing. A harmless token that will surely come of no need to you. A small price to pay to have your beloved in your arms again."

She stood in disbelief, knowing she could not go on without her love. Staring with longing and need, she processed the visitor's offer in her head. His gift would give her back the thing she treasured most in the world. She knew what she would need to do.

She gave a single nod, to the unknown caller. He reciprocated with a coy grin in his eyes. She fell abruptly to her knees, her head facing the sky. Ethereal mist billowed from inside her toward the ceiling, a violent volcano erupting her precious gift from her mouth. Fog filled the room enveloping them, swirling in circles then moved as if pulled by a vacuum into a small velveteen box resting in the visitor's outstretched hands.

The stranger snapped the box shut and closed the gold latch. He had collected his coveted bounty. With a cunning smile, he stepped back, satisfied with his gift. He gave a silent bow, disappearing into the shadows just as swiftly as he had arrived.

She heard a soft moan and turned her attention back to her beloved. The body of her fallen betrothed stirred as he opened his eyes. She sat at his side in disbelief. He had returned to her. He looked to her with a loving gaze, his heart warm with adoration. It was as if he were seeing her beauty for the first time.

She took his hand in hers, but no tears escaped from her eyes. She had been given back her One; the Inferno would have no guests that night. Her lips parted and she attempted to declare proclamations of devotion, but only silence escaped. Again, she tried to cry out in joy, but words had escaped her. She could only sit and stare into his eyes with cold silence.

The soft pattern of her heartbeat ceased to dance. Her chest now only contained a stone hollow. Where she once felt love, now only an empty void lived. She looked into the eyes of her waking beloved and felt the coldness of detachment. His smiling face elicited no sense of relief within, she cared not that he had come back to her. Ardor turned to apathy. Adoration had been replaced with indifference.

She realized was in her soul that love lived, and by abiding by the stranger's request she gave away her only ability to feel the one thing she had prayed for. Satan's Salesman had given her the cruelest of gifts; her animus in exchange for an eternal life of being unable to love with her hollow heart.

She cried for the stranger to return, begged to an empty room to take back her offer. How could she punish her beloved with an eternity of rejection? But she knew, her symbolic signature was iron clad; there was no return policy. Her fate had been written in irony through desire, the price of her request had been paid in full.

Her love looked into her eyes, exuding the passion she could only dream about now. With an empty heart and detached voice she spoke...

MirroRED

by Amanda Mueller

My mind goes blank when the men in the scarlet lab coats restrain me to a frigid gurney. I try to move my hands, but they remain glued to the padding like a piece of gum under a student's desk. The ceiling tiles move rapidly above me making my head spin in circles. I notice these men's faces are masked by shadows withholding me from making out what they look like. My brittle lips move in an effort to call out for help, but no sound makes it past the boundaries of my imagination. I hear metal objects clank together to what I can only assume are medical instruments being prepared. A needle filled with blue liquid comes into my field of vision along with the face of one of the men whose smile couldn't cover any more of his face if he tried to.

"Don't be afraid. You're about to save millions of lives, all for the measly price of one."

My eyes jolt open as I wake up in a cold sweat, trying to regain my thoughts of what's actually real and what was just a dream. I wipe my face and feel tears staining my temples. With a sigh, I sit up and gradually remember the present to which I compare to Armageddon. I still wonder why these dreams have felt so real recently. It's almost as if for that short time I want soundless sleep, my head decides to make up whatever irrational scenario it can conjure just to purposely scare me. At this point, I'm used to it.

I hurriedly shove the case files I've been studying every night into my backpack and pick up my journal. The bookmark made out of a crumpled newspaper article marks the page where I wrote my last entry. Might as well keep track of all the ludicrous events happening as proof for when the next generation of kids calls my bluff. I know they won't put any of this on public record since I'm pretty sure killing your own people would be frowned upon. According to this newspaper article, some insane scientist went rogue which started the pandemic we're in all because he was experimenting on viruses. It's unnerving to me how blindly people trust our "beloved" government even when the only thing coming from the lips of these men are blunt lies. Apparently blaming these deaths on everyone and everything but themselves is considered good leadership.

My last journal entry talks about the lockdown that was ordered nationwide only days ago. No one's allowed outside of their own homes until further notice because it's considered unsafe. Some people don't believe in the lies while others swear it's hard facts as if they've been brainwashed. I don't know where I stand on this argument, or at least I didn't. The more I dig up from this whole scandal, the more I become dumbfounded on how it all comes down to one person taking the blame.

I stupidly can't help but keep wondering what happened to him. To the boy I've known for only two years yet feels more like a lifetime. We're strangers really since he's just the lab boy who used to take my blood for the doctor. Although he did jeopardize himself to help me. More than once. Our last fight replays in the back of my mind and for a moment, my chest burns up.

"You're not listening to me, Ellie. These boneheads will do anything to prove their loyalty to the Nation, even if it means turning their backs on their own brothers." His voice rose with every word that came from his mouth making his face red, yet his eyes remained glossy the entire conversation. I was sitting with my legs dangling over a hospital bed, my arms crossed refusing to listen to his nonsense. I remember barely looking at him as if he were a stranger. He doesn't know what he's talking about. If only I put aside my ego long enough to hear him out, maybe I could've heard the plea for help in his hoarse voice. That was the day he crossed the line. He broke whatever protocols that were in place to restrain him from telling me his real feelings.

"I hear you, Marshall. I just don't believe you." My words came out in a whisper, worried they would sting him. He had told me everything he knew about the deaths, the spores, the immaculate plans in store for our country. Basically how the government plans to use this deadly disease that sprung out of nowhere to control the population how they see fit. Portraying propaganda on the news about how they will find a cure and fix this. Marshall told me that this "cure" is all for show. Once it's released to the public after testing, there will be no one left except for the few who are immune.

I can't believe that he's telling the truth. It sounds ridiculous. "Why would the government want us all dead? They don't even have proof of people being immune, it makes no sense." It's all mere speculation to me. That only made the blood in his pale face deepen.

"Ellie. . . please." Our eyes met, and I could see that there was something else he wasn't saying. I remember the doctor came in and wrapped up my routine checkup, interrupting our little argument. His eyes stayed on me while the doctor discussed how everything was good and I was set to go back home. The doctor added how my labs still appeared abnormal, but it's no cause for alarm since I still appear healthy overall.

All I could think about was how I wanted to get out of there, far away dismissing his accusations. As I left down the hall, his voice echoed while he fought the guards taking him into custody. That was the last time I saw him. If he's right, there won't be much left of this place soon.

According to these possibly stolen case files, the selected individuals who agreed to participate in the Viral Trials are all deceased. This makes sense since all past attempts at a cure are nonexistent but still doesn't explain why these people are dead.

Scientifically speaking, if a scientist fails an experiment, don't they start over and try again? There's no record of another trial anywhere that I could find. Funny how the participant's deaths are nowhere to be found either like it never happened.

Logged in the back of each file lies a section vividly explaining how each participant died. I've tried to make sense of it a few times before giving up completely. Something about mutated proteins and gene therapy gone wrong. Scientific lingo just isn't my thing. Hopefully, I'll be able to get some useful answers from them, but so far, just headaches.

The one thing each of these files has in common is the signature of a guy named Peter Hayes. The same guy from my newspaper article.

I finish stuffing my backpack and toss it over my shoulder. If I have to spend one more day surrounded by these same four walls while my fingers become stuck scrolling through my phone for endless hours, my brain might turn into jello.

Since the lockdown, people's living arrangements have been adjusted to accommodate the government's needs. People who live in houses were assigned a zone where they receive their supplies along with daily checkups in case of any new outbreaks. People like me, on the other hand, who live in apartment buildings are subject to living like prisoners. Locked inside with no control of our own lives except for the decision of whether to have tacos or pasta for dinner. All the apartment buildings are infested with security guards since they've turned each building into their little bases. No one may be allowed in or out of their rooms without clearance from certified personnel, but that hasn't stopped me from finding my way around the system.

I live on the 7th floor of a fourteen-story building, which makes for a beautiful view from the top. The guards rotate shifts around eight every night leaving certain floors unattended for a short period of time. I pace outside my door waiting for the elevator shaft to mark my cue, giving me that small dosage of freedom. I wonder if people felt this overwhelming sense of freedom almost every day before life became so constricted or if that feeling goes away once you have it so often. Taken for granted. I smirk at myself. I guess anything can be taken for granted if you have enough of it. Even people. You always think they'll be there, forever. Until one day they're saying all the wrong things creating this huge gap. And it feels like there's no way to close it because it's grown too wide without even realizing it.

All the pain-shattering emotions that you shoved into this little box get cut open with no way of closing it back up. You feel it all at once wondering how you ever took them for granted in the first place. Or people just die for no good reason. Same difference.

An odd feeling washes over me. I wonder if Marshall would appreciate a freeing view.

The elevator creaks its way up to my floor with a ding announcing the doors are opening. That's my cue. I push open my apartment door to get a peek down the wide hallway.

Four guards dressed in an absurd amount of black gear begin briefing each other on any crucial events that occurred throughout their day. The one with aviator sunglasses resting on his shaved head tells the others about a group of kids caught partying together in one of the red zones.

One of the other guys, with a full-grown beard, shakes his head while the rest of them snicker. I roll my eyes.

The bearded guy shushes their immature behavior and tells them something I can't quite make out. He's talking in a whisper, and the others seem to have a serious look on their faces again.

They all head around the corner out of my sight to settle in for their shift, still talking in hushed tones.

I take advantage of their disappearance and stagger to the end of the hall where I push through the door leading up to the roof. My feet tap against the metal steps urging me to hurry, but my head tells me to stop. Something's bugging me about the way they all turned so serious. I head back down and crack the door open slightly. Two of the guards step onto the elevator, one holding the door open to listen to their last order from the bearded guy.

"When you get down to the basement floor, take into account all the ones who showed no symptoms. They are being requested for transfer to Green Zone B. The ones who are positive stay here to be taken care of."

The two on the elevator nod in unison and stand back with their arms folded behind them, fading away behind the double doors. Bearded guy and his partner, who remains eerily quiet, go to sit in their chairs, both now lost in their phones.

I start climbing my way back up to the roof, but can't stop wondering what he meant by that. The way he said "taken care of" doesn't sound like something good. Sounds more like what a monster would say to his live meal to calm them down before devouring every last piece of them. A shiver runs down my spine. Why would they transfer people to another zone? I thought it wasn't safe to be outside unless absolutely necessary due to the spores being highly contagious. Why would they risk exposing those people? They would need some sort of escorts to expose too. Their own men. It doesn't add up. I get that going outside doesn't automatically make you sick as some people think. Those people are the ones you see wearing gas masks before they even step out of their front door. Then again, you never know -

My body gets pushed into the wall as I trip and tumble down what feels like a whole flight of stairs. My heart starts pounding against my chest while all the pressure from my head feels light. I start to shout at whoever pushed me but get cut off by a boy's voice.

"Sorry! Sorry, I didn't mean to shove you that hard." His voice cracked in the middle of his sentence, making me assume he's about thirteen years old. "Something's going on upstairs, top floor. My friend told me to come. Like now."

"What?" I clench my jaw and don't even bother to hide the bluntness in my voice. Before he can answer, a ton of people barge into the stairwell shuffling up the stairs in a rush like people during a Black Friday Sale.

"The guards left their posts! Hurry if you want to see it!"

If I want to see what? Why are the guards gone? I get up and start racing up the stairs, pushing my way through the sea of people. No one's mouth is moving but the taps of our shoes against the steps combined together make a deafening sound.

Once we all make it to the top, I realize there are a lot fewer people than I imagined. Only about nine of us. I know certain people who would jump at any opportunity to leave their rooms. Living in an apartment building is like having a dysfunctional family you never asked for or didn't think you wanted. I don't recognize anyone.

I stand next to the boy who ran into me on the stairs. "So… where's everyone else?" His eyes stay glued to the horizon as if something spectacular is about to happen. The moonlight casts a glow on his figure, outlining what looks like needle marks trailing his forearm.

"I'm not sure. Must not have gotten the memo." His tone gives my stomach an uneasy feeling as if he knows all of our tragic fates. "You never know when you'll get your last tomorrow. When all you can do is gaze forward with no meaning left. When they take everything from you without a moment's consideration. Like human life doesn't even matter."

He looks at me in the eyes for the first time, and that's when I see it. A green haze clouds his innocent eyes like a scientist who's gone mentally insane. The vein above his right eye pulses with green and black as if someone stained his skin on purpose. Despite his sickly appearance, his face remains emotionless and unbothered by my wide eyes. He must have looked like this for a while if he's used to soundless reactions like mine.

Before another word can be spoken between us, a blinding light emits from one of the red zones below us. My hands cover my eyes before my brain can process the chaos that unfolds in front of me.

A memory jolts through my mind from science class about light traveling faster than sound. It's considered a cold, hard fact, but you don't understand it because you would think they would happen at the exact same time. It makes more sense that way. It's the loud boom that comes next that makes me realize science was right. All of the houses, the tents, the people… gone within a matter of seconds. Blue flames remain the only source of light left after the explosion dies down. To my surprise, the kids around me aren't shocked one bit. Almost like they knew it was going to happen.

An eerie silence settles in the room around us until another thunderous sound goes off somewhere in the distance to what I can only imagine is another zone blown to pieces. My hands begin to shake and my lungs can't seem to find enough air. I need to get out of here.

I sprint back down the stairs building up a sweat. I have zero idea where I'm going to go, but anywhere is better than waiting around for a possible death sentence. I decide to stop on my floor and take the elevator the rest of the way down, putting my trust in those crazed kids' words about the guards going AWOL. My mind goes back to the kid with the messed up eyes. It's on the tip of my tongue, but I can't fully make out where I've read something like that before. And the countless scars on his arm like he had a bunch of tests done to him. Makes me sick thinking someone cold enough could do that to a helpless kid. I'm so fed up with this jacked-up system we call our government. Like we're all spawns waiting to be used in their demented games.

I reach the elevator with no one to stop me thankfully and step inside it. My body stands still, yet every nerve in my body is jittering in anticipation for whatever is about to unravel once those doors open.

The number above the silver doors read number five. My heart thumps against my chest. I haven't been in the lobby of this building in I can't even remember how long. Excitement surges through me oddly enough.

Number three.

Being able to breathe fresh air and feel the dirt beneath my feet again instead of fuzzy carpets and musty air all trapped with nowhere to go. It almost makes me forget the reason I'm forced to be here in the first place.

Number two.

I take a slow, deep breath in trying to calm my body down. Sometimes we have to take risks in order to drive ourselves forward and grow. Number one flashes across the screen, but the elevator continues moving down. My heart stops. I pressed the main floor button, I know I did.

The elevator comes to a halt with a dinging noise announcing its arrival at its supposed destination. The doors open to a dark room lit only by a blue glow that encases what seem to be, glass cages. I step onto the concrete floor and look around for a proper light switch. The elevator closes making me jump and begins its ascension, leaving me alone with nothing but the blue glow to guide me through the darkness. My eyes gradually become accustomed to my restricted vision, and I find a light switch on the wall closest to me. I flip it on making my eyes squint and my jaw drops shortly after in response to what lies in this room.

More kids, all in separate cages. There's a ton of medical equipment crowding every space possible along with screens covering an entire wall. I walk over to see bedrooms on every screen, but not one person in view. I notice artwork painted across one of the walls of the bedrooms. Roses mixed with hearts growing together with my name signed near the top of a rose petal.

My apartment.

There's a green piece of tape on the top of this monitor along with a few others, but there's also ones marked with red tape. Like the red zones that got destroyed. My mouth feels dry all of a sudden. Why are they watching us like lab rats? Why does a basement like this exist in apartment buildings? How come no one ever noticed? If they're using us all for some grand scheme, what did they do to Marshall? I should've listened to him when I had the chance. He could actually be dead for all I know. How could I fail him like this?

I turn back and try to focus on figuring out how to help the kids who are still here. I go over to the cages wondering if there's a way to help them out of their worst nightmare. Keypads make up the handles of the glass doors, asking for a four-digit code. My eyes trace the tubing that's hooked up to them like puppets. I wonder what kind of drugs they've been prescribed, my brain always leading me to the worst-case scenario. It's unnerving to me why all of the kids appear to be sleeping so peacefully. I push away that bad thought immediately.

There's a younger girl in one of the glass cubes, huddled in a ball with her light hair falling around her thin face. She's holding onto a little pink stuffed animal, probably using it as her security blanket thinking it makes her invincible from anything. Reminds me of my younger sister who used to hold onto me at night whenever she got scared I might've left her. That's the kind of fear you get when you're little and your parents ship you off to another country because it's "safer" there instead of being afraid of monsters in your closet.

I jump back a bit when I hear a thud come from behind me. The blood in my skin burns up and restricts me from turning around as if a monster may really be towering over me. I half-open my eyes and slowly turn my body around, hoping the sound was just my imagination. That's when our eyes meet. Even in the dark, I recognize those piercing blue eyes anywhere.

"Ellie?"

I stand there like a fool frozen in a dumb video game, not able to fully comprehend that he's standing right in front of me obstructed by only a thin wall of glass. My heart burns up suddenly matching the color of my face, but fades away as quickly as it came. His hair clings to his forehead, and his stupid side smile shines up his entire face. That smile tugs at my heart every time I see it.

"How did you get down here? The explosions, I thought you were. . ." His voice trails off and I know how he was about to end that sentence. His smile fades away, replaced with a serious expression. I walk closer to the glass as if to prove that I'm perfectly fine.

"I'm okay Marshall. Those explosions were targeted towards red zones. Not this one to my understanding." I have a million questions to ask him, as I'm sure he does too. My mind can't seem to stop spinning to focus on a specific one that would be beneficial to our given circumstance. I take notice of him fiddling with the tubs connected to his forearm which makes me frown. Scientists really do obsess too much over things they shouldn't be.

Marshall taps on the glass, pointing to one of the countertops. "The keycard should be in one of those drawers. And bring scissors over too. I want these bloodsuckers to stop using me as a food bank."

I search through the drawers full of more tubes and medicines until I see a shiny card with a chip in it. Bingo. I grab what looks like shears, and hurry back over to his door. The rest of these kids better be alive.

I swipe the card against the metal pad to which the door releases a clicking sound, swinging it open. We both stand there for a moment, looking at each other without speaking a word. I want to tell him how sorry I was for not hearing him out better and getting him set up as the government's guinea pig. I want to wrap my arms around him and never let him go again as if he might disappear on me any second. But I decided against all of those things, worried it might come across the wrong way. Besides, he's just the boy who used to take my blood.

I hand him the shears and watch him cut the tubes connecting him to a big pool of blue liquid. He goes over to a table to clean up and tape the opening that's left of the tube. I run over to the other glass cubes in hopes of saving the others, but Marshall protests against that.

"Don't open those. They. . . they lost to the spores, Ellie. I'm sorry. They aren't human anymore." He goes back to fixing himself up as if that was common knowledge to him. Didn't even bat an eye.

"Are you sure? There's a little girl in this one and she-"

"She's gone. I'm sorry." He finishes his bandaging and comes over to me with his eyes glossy. "She was the first one they manipulated as part of their trial experiments. Dosed her up with what I'm assuming is a makeshift vaccine against the spores. Her body couldn't handle it. That was a couple of weeks ago."

His voice turned soft, and I can see how much of a toll being down here like this took on him. I tiptoe around this subject as best I can. "Do you know what they're planning to do because wiping out the whole population just seems ridiculous if you ask me?" His eyes stay fixated on the girl.

"They've been trying to find the source of this whole mess, and I've heard they narrowed it down to one person. Just one person. Some lame genetic disorder, and instead of working up a way to fix it, they decided to use the person as a bio-weapon for the war effort. No one knows where this person is though, or who for that matter. The government covered it all up. What a shocker. As for the spores that mutated from that person, they're too strong for our bodies to handle according to Mister Obvious who set up these crucial tests. So they've been trying to create something that could fight it. Something stronger than us, but you know scientists always find a way to royally screw up."

My heart sinks deep in my chest. "Where is this thing now?"

He runs his fingers through his hair as if that helps him think straighter. "Gone."

That wasn't the response I was expecting. I start to ask what he meant by that but get cut off by the little girl who was supposedly dead pounding against the glass doors. Her eyes are wide open and full of that same green color that the other boy had on the roof. The noises coming from her mouth are inhumane. I jump out of my skin, but Marshall remains completely still as if expecting that to happen. "We have to go before they remember that their most prized possessions are here."

I glare at him."What do you mean by that?" The girl keeps using her fists to try to pry open the door with no success.

"Ellie, you really don't know, do you?" The way he's talking sounds like he's practiced that sentence for this moment. All the hairs on the back of my neck rise up.

"Just tell me." That comes out harsher than I intended it to.

"You've been exposed to the spores and this new, accidental invention created by these mad scientists. You haven't turned yet. They've been pumping me with this virus for weeks. I'm still me."

I don't move my gaze off him and wait for him to just spit it out. He lets out an exaggerated sigh. "We're immune Ellie, and everyone wants our blood. The government realized how much they messed up with the rest of its people though. And they want to start over, like none of this ever happened."

I gulp at how calm he seems to be about this. "Start over? Do I even want to know?" My voice comes out in a whisper.

"Probably not. . . but it doesn't matter. What does is they've started Operation Eschatology. They want to wipe out everyone who isn't immune."

Just as he finishes talking, another earth-shattering boom comes from above us. He pulls me to him, covering my body, and we both fall to the floor. When the boom quiets down, we both look up to see nothing but a blue sky full of smoke. The building's just gone like some twisted magic trick. Soldiers dressed in all white peer over the edges of the new hole, staring at us like we're live prey. My ears are still ringing from the explosion which makes it impossible for me to know if they're talking to us or not. Before I'm able to recompose myself, one of the men in white makes his way down by some sort of machine and starts pulling Marshall off of me. I try to protest but another one kicks me down, making me roll over in pain.

A woman emerges from the crowd looking me dead in the eyes as if she's been waiting for this moment her whole life. A white dress falls loosely around her, covered by a military jacket painted in the same color. Her soldiers follow in foot behind her, their guns all pointed on me with their fingers inches away from the trigger daring me to make a move.

"So, you're the one with the genetic mutation who caused the nationwide pandemic."

THE DEVIL'S PROMISE

By Jennifer Jennings Daves

Reuben watched her from a distance. He knew better than to disturb Mara when she was out on the rocks. He hated himself for it. The reason she sat out there and wailed the night away. The fog was coming in thicker tonight, but he kept watch; focusing on her lantern to keep a fix on her position. All the while, running the events of last year through his mind. Could he have done anything differently? Should he have refused Tom a place on his crew? He had no way of knowing that storm would come. No way of knowing that the mast would snap like a twig, tossing the crow's nest right into the craggy rocks. It took the better part of a week for Tom's storm-wracked body to wash back ashore.

When his body was first found, Mara went into such a grievous shock that she went into early labor. Three days later, she found herself burying both husband and son. Ever since then, she has walked the rocks; singing like a siren in the hopes that it will bring them all together again.

He is always afraid she will slip herself into the cold northern waters so that she can sleep forever with those she loves. His guilt haunting him, he shifts his position so that he can see her better. Two small stones cascade down to the water, barely making a sound. But it was enough to cause Mara to jump to her feet.

"Show yourself!" She screamed. "I know you're watching me, Reuben Crisp!"

She quickly scrambles to a higher rock, shining her lantern towards the shore.

Sighing, Reuben hoisted himself to his feet, or foot as the case was, as he had lost the one to frostbite as a young lad. The grief was hard for him to bear too. Tom wasn't just his chosen first mate for that fateful fishing trip. He was his baby brother. The one he saved from freezing to death the winter he lost his leg.

Mara came barreling up to him. She looked like a water fairy next to his six-foot-four massive built frame. God! How he adored her! But he dare not let her know. He had stayed silent when she chose his brother. He had stayed silent all this year. Yet he wanted to tell her that he had loved her from the moment her mom had let him hold her when she was no more than a newborn babe. He had promised then that he would always watch out for her and he planned on making good on that promise. So far, it was the only one he had been able to keep.

"What gives you the right to spy on me in my grief!" she demanded as she slammed her tiny fists into his chest.

He would take all her anger if it could bring them back.

"I just wanted to make sure you made it back to shore safely, Mara." he looked away as he spoke, lest she sees the tears welling up in his eyes.

How could he tell her of his love for her? After everything that had happened between them.

"Why do you care if I make it back or not? You probably wish I was dead too!" she wailed as the tears streamed down her face.

Did she dare tell him the truth? That she loved him. That she always had. She regretted marrying Tom. He had been a cruel husband. He blamed her for his shortcomings and inability to be a real man. He came close to strangling the life out of her one night. But he left her on the floor, gasping for breath.

When she awoke the next morning, he was gone. She didn't see him for days. Then he came home with a man she had never seen before.

"I found him, Mara, my love!" he declared.

"Found who?" she asked.

"The man that can be the father for our children." He stared at her with hardened eyes as he watched the realization of his words sink into her heart. He then quietly turned and bolted the door and sat in a chair. He watched as the man took his wife.

He watched for hours until Mara finally screamed in agonizing pain. Then he grabbed the wretch of a man up and tossed him out the back door and his clothes after him.

Tom then tossed a rag in her direction.

"Now go wash yourself, you worthless whore!" He shouted while opening a fresh bottle of whiskey.

Then the wait began. But the answer didn't take long to reveal itself. Within two months they both knew she was with child. The whole village was overjoyed at the happy news.

Even Reuben seemed overjoyed, saying he couldn't wait to become uncle Reub. She slowly started to die inside. She knew the bargain her husband had made with that devil. He would be back in two years. And now one and a half had passed.

Dare she tell Reuben the truth? That his brother had been a devil? Would he believe her? Would he protect her from the devil to come? She was afraid to find out. She was afraid she really was all alone in the world. Her parents were dead. Her brother and his wife lived far away and her sister was a maid with no way to help her out.

"Mara", Reuben's quiet and defeated voice brought her back to reality. "Would you care for some tea?"

It was only then that she realized that they had walked all the way back to her cottage.

Mara nodded her head and was grateful to warn her hands by wrapping them tight around the mug full of steaming hot tea. They sat in silence for what seemed an eternity. The only sounds were the clock ticking away on the wall and the distant crash of the waves below. Mara and Tom's cottage sat perched on the cliff that looked out over the bay. They could sit on the front porch and gaze across and watch the townspeople go about their daily business.

Now Reuben was standing and putting on his coat and hat.

"I know things are hard right now, Mara," Reuben said. "But I promise to help as much as I can. The fishing season is about to start again and the ship has a full crew. I won't allow you to starve."

He stared out past the rocks to the far side of the bay.

"Hopefully, the weather will remain fair and we will have good sailing."

With that, he donned his cap and walked out the door which Mara promptly bolted shut.

She then gratefully sank into her bed and fell asleep.

Mara watched the ship leave the harbor two days later. She was, once again, totally alone with her thoughts. She stared out at the ocean wondering what would be the best for her to do. Should she end it all while Reuben was out to sea or just pack up and leave?

"Mara!" Hearing her name bolted her back to reality. Her sister, Megan, had come for a visit. "I need your help, sister," she said. "The upstairs maid quit and the Davenports need a replacement right now."

Mara saw this as an opportunity. She could earn money to leave Watertown for good. Then maybe, that devil would never find her and she would be safe. So, she packed her stuff and moved in with Megs.

Reuben was both shocked and pleased at the news when they got back to port after three weeks at sea. It had been a truly successful trip. Their catch fetched quite a pretty price at the market in Boston. Not only had he been able to pay his crew well, but he had money enough to pay the final payment on the headstones for his brother and nephew. Both of which, were being put in place at the graveyard.

Things seemed to be going quite well. Maybe he and Mara could move past their mutual pain of loss and forge ahead together. They both secretly hoped this, but only time would tell if the devil would ruin the plans of the heart.

TIME TO FLY

by Brandy Lane

Still meandering down rivers of thought from lucid dreams from the night prior, a hazy morn of afterthoughts linger in my mind. I snuggle down into the sheets, not quite ready to leave my slumber. The glow of morning tries to pry my eyes open, but blankets make a good shield. I settle into the dark comfort, cozy and warm.

Peacefully cocooned, I become one with the bed, like we are liquid. My body can no longer feel pain or pressure, I just am. Swirling colors fill my head, a hunger for sweets, a need for fragrance on the winds of fresh air. In my mind, I fly above the earth, on wings like paper... fluttering so high, as to brush the currents above. I can feel the air push me around, much like turbulence I have felt before while flying in an airplane.

My mouth is dry, I try to moisten it by swirling my tongue around in my mouth to no avail. I catch a whiff of sweetness, the nectar I have been craving. I drift down in circles, slowly like a feather, no effort is needed for this, I am just enjoying the ride. I see fields of clover below me, the perfume is exquisite; honey-sweet and intoxicating. I take my fill of the nectar before me. Satiated now, I rest for a while on the stems of the blooms that I've just imbibed. I leave behind my legacy, eggs for a new generation to carry on my tradition of floating on the wind and drinking the most tantalizing concoctions that nature has crafted. I fly off on the breeze, my job complete. I fly over a pond to see my last reflection and become lunch for a snapping turtle.

My body still in bed, I toss and turn within my sheets, still deep within my dream, my eyes are rapidly moving, as I slip into the abyss of REM. My mind is anywhere but with my body.

A feeling comes over me, as I am once again without wings, but am eating the leaves of the plant that I have just quenched my thirst from. I am not sure how this has happened, or where my wings have gone, perhaps they were the dreams of the creature that I now inhabit? Munching and munching, I eat and eat and eat until I can barely move. Eat and eat and eat and eat and eat. The chewing sounds are so loud in my head, but it is all I can do to relieve the feeling I have inside.

In reality, I am grinding my teeth down in my sleep, wearing them down to a shine.

Tangled in my sheets, it is getting much harder to move. I succumb, my head still covered to keep out the light. I am paralyzed in my entanglement, barely able to breathe. Unaware of my current state, I continue to dream.

In my dream, I realize that I am, indeed, a caterpillar. In my subconscious state, I have accepted that after my last demise of the snapping turtle, I have somehow reincarnated through one of the eggs that I had previously laid. My body is now bloated, I am exhausted. With all of the energy left within my being, I move my corpulent body up the side of a child's abandoned swing set and hang upside down. My body is encapsulated slowly, by a glistening, hardening shell. On the outside of the shell, are tiny gold dots; a gold rim, worn like a crown. I am a king, I am a monarch!

Inside of my shell, I am primordial goo, my body aches as I cannot move, yet my cells are moving on their very own, transforming my body and mind to be something completely different than just an eating machine. I am slowly being reconstructed into a completely different being, a new energy source, a new life. A miracle is happening inside of that tiny shell, what looks like it could be my final resting place, is becoming a place of rebirth, renewal, and regrowth.

Not sure of how much time has passed, I awake in my chrysalis, trying to stretch and move, and burst out of my confined space. I writhe for what seems like hours, I am hot and sweaty, and desperate to escape. I try to chew through my could-be tomb, where I'm not able to extract myself. I cannot breathe, I lie there, unable to find the strength to move.

In real-time, my breath has slowed, I am still in a very deep sleep and unaware that I am breathing in my own expired carbon dioxide trapped within the blanket covering my head. My dream is trying to tell me to awaken, but I am so weak, that I cannot move. My mind, not quite thinking properly in its oxygen-deprived state, uses what strength it has left to help the butterfly escape.

All of my resources go to my dreams, all I can think about is how the butterfly needs to be free!

It just has to make it!

I channel my energy to that of the monarch. I push and writhe and chew and stretch, and finally, break free of my prison. I unfurl my wings, wet and crumpled, and unable to fly and I rest.

After a bit, I spread my wings, the hunger and thirst drive me to awaken to my new life, no longer encumbered by my corpulent body, no longer trapped within my own boundaries. I start off on a new journey, to drift along on the windy currents, to fly up to the heavens, to look down on the world below in search of the sweet nectar of life. I flutter up to the ceiling, unable to go any further.

I stop and rest, and look below.

I see a foot, my foot, sticking out from the bottom of the covers on the bed. The human form that I had once taken, is motionless; breathing has ceased.

Desperate to awaken, I flutter down to tickle my feet, to no avail.

I was discovered a few hours later when my husband arrived home to surprise me for our anniversary. He discovered my body, trapped within the sheets, suffocated. It seems I had tried to chew my way out of them in my sleep. He tried to resuscitate me, but I had already gone, already flown. I fluttered down onto the cocoon that I once inhabited.

In his sorrow, he picked me up and held me close. He did not notice the butterfly that had landed on my chest. I could feel him, hear his loud heartbeat as he held my human form for the very last time. Before I could realize what was truly happening, I heard my wings crumbling around me from the weight of our bodies being compressed. I couldn't yell or scream, I couldn't fly, I couldn't...

I REMEMBER JEAN

by CA Newry

I remember the look that he gave me the last time I spoke to him. It was creepy; disturbing, to say the least. I remember his stare seemed void of emotion. It was simply a blank look that seemed absent of self: a complete withdrawal from reality. At this moment, I remember Jean seeming lost to me; he was emotionally disconnected from where I stood talking to him. I remember desperately wanting to help him; wanting to reach out and fix him; this wasn't the boy I went to school with; this human shell wasn't the man I worked 7 plus years within a luxury resort dealing with VIP clients; where was the man who went out of his way in order to ensure that I was safely dropped off home after long-ass work shifts at nights?

So I asked him, "Jean, what the hell is wrong with you? You're about to get freaking written up. Catch you're freaking self."

As I write, I remember him slowly turning to face me; face contorted and sweating profusely. I remember him leaning towards me to whisper,

"Cecil, Jean is no longer here."

Then there was silence. No more words from him. He completely ignored me, staring at the computer screen that had already blanked out, fallen to sleep due to un-use. I remember thinking, *well mudda Etel, Jean is freaking possessed. I am in this butler pantry with a gaddamn demon and the mudda flipping pantry door locked. Where the hell is Derek?*

Moments before this exchange, Jean and Derek had a heated argument. It was so heated that Derek, who was the butler assistant manager, frantically cleared the entire butler pantry of its occupants; abruptly ending our afternoon briefing. Derek planned to *deal* with Jean for his public and blatantly insubordination. I saw the contemptuous look in Derek's eyes for our friend; remembering our journey within this department, I begged for a chance to intervene. Derek relented, due to our friendship and stormed out, promising to return to *finish* his discussion with Jean in 5 minutes.

Derek, Jean, and I were amongst the last of the original butlers at the Ocean Club. There were about 6 of us now out of the total 25 VIP butlers. The three of us were trained by Sir Ashley Powel and Ivory Spencer; distinguished English gentlemen and butler in the household of the English Royal family. Our skill set was rare and sought after locally and internationally. One just cannot *deal* with a gentleman any kind of way; thus I felt compelled to intervene for principal sake.

Truth is, for a while Jean had not been acting himself. He had distanced himself from his colleagues and friends. He was no longer jovial in nature; he was always serious and always in a hurry. He had a number of unexplained verbal outbursts with staff and management. He quoted Biblical scriptures that were dark in nature and always recanted strange quotes from unknown sourcebooks he called 'hidden knowledge'. For some reason, he wanted to chant down Babylon and save the Bahamas from the pending tribulation. He was terrified that the Bahamas would be taken over by the pale-faced, blue-eyed devils who endeavored to re-enslaved the Negros; and at every opportunity, he would admonish anyone who was idle enough to listen, to see tourism as a continuation of the plantation system.

Jean also had a few guest's complaints about his perpetual, unflinching stares. A few female guests made casual passing remarks that it seemed as if Jean was staring at them behind his dark glasses. Sitting here, I remember that this incident had to have been late August 2001. It was freaking hot as ass. I remember we all packed extra t-shirts and deodorant at work in order to maintain ourselves. Butlers had to maintain standards of excellence despite the harsh conditions. The Ocean Club resort rooms were all spaced out, outside cottages; subsequently, we all had to trod through the elements in order to serve the guests. *I hated this shit; as for some strange ass reason, hotel guests always decide to want ice to be brought to their rooms when torrential rains would fall and many a time I had to service a room with my clothes drenched with water.* This summer, the butlers got permission to wear sunglasses like the beach and pool attendants due to the blazing sun rays...but this quickly ended due to Jean's antics.

Jean refused to take his sunglasses off even when he was inside, speaking to management, or even when he was servicing guests. He refused to reveal his eyes, citing to me once, that "the eyes were the window of the soul; that he must protect his soul from the devils". I am not sure where he got that sassy talk from; but once, I had spotted Jean alone in the hotel's guests' computer lab, with every damn light off, sitting at a computer watching YouTube videos about the reptilian race. Even then, in the dark, he wore his dark shades. I remember making a motion to caution him, but the gaze he gave me forced me to reconsider my action and carry my ass along, having me conclude to myself, *management in the future ga have to deal with that crazy ass.*

So now I am back at the pantry, Derek reentered its quarters calmer, but still eager to *deal* with Jean. But before he motioned to pull him aside, I whispered with tears in my eyes, "buey Derek, wait, this bitch crazy to ratid. I think you should forward this shit to H.R."

Jean continued sitting upright and still, staring at the blank computer screen, motionless, not once looking up at us, as we discussed him. If my memory serves me correctly, Derek sent Jean home that evening in order for him to calm his nerves. By chance, Jean had another additional 2 days off according to the scheduled roster and this gave Derek time to find a solution to this potential vexing issue. But it was too late.

Mind you, I too was off the next day, so what I am about to say here now, is purely here say, recanted to me by butlers who were at work that day. Apparently on his day off, Jean returned to work frantically wanting to retrieve his Bible. *I forgot to mention earlier, Jean touted a bible with him every gaddamn where he went.* Apparently, he had left it in the butler's pantry.

At the security gate, Jean parked his truck. (I remember that truck; we all envied him for it. It was beyond our salary's reach; it was a baller's truck and Jean took pride in maintaining and cleaning his prize daily. In the middle of a shift he would wipe her down in the parking lot).

In any event, Jean had left Pookie, his girlfriend, and his 4-month-old baby in the truck. *Pookie was another one of Jean's prizes; they had just recently moved in with each other some months before, in a high-end apartment out East near the canals. Pookie was one pretty ass girl: a Nikki Manaj look alike. She was built like a brick and Jean jealously guarded her.* It was during the short seconds of Jean's departure from the truck, *they* say that Pookie exited the automobile and desperately ran with her child to the resort's gate security officer for help; pleading with him to save her, to save them. When Jean returned, seeing Pookie missing, he flipped. Searching the immediate area, seeing her speaking to the security officer, he violently charged after them, spitting out cuss words, accusing the love of his life of betrayal, accusing her of having relations with the now confused officer. Jean demanded to have his baby. Pookie refused; a physical scuffle ensued and the infant dropped in the street bawling. The security had to save the baby, as Jean chased his woman down the street.

Needless to say Jean and Pookie separated. Rumor has that he stalked her ass for days afterward. She had to go into hiding for a while. Jean was fired from Ocean Club on his day off. No one heard from him in weeks. September 11th came and went. America was under attack by terrorists. Tourism came to a standstill in the Bahamas. We all were terrified for our jobs. For the first time in history, mid-management went on days as occupancy went down to single digits. Paradise Island was a ghost town and talks about mass layoffs loomed. The entire world had changed as America became afraid of its shadow.

Then, Jean reappeared. Somehow, Jean had bypassed Bahamian police, airport security, and U.S. TSA guards, gaining access and entry into the U.S. Customs section of the Nassau International Airport. There, he adorned the same blue trench coat he wore all the time at the Ocean Club and the dark sunglasses, grabbing hold of a US customs agent....he shouted, "Everyone on the fucking ground, this is a terrorist attack!"

Of course, this put the airport on high alert. When the U.S. customs agent began to scream, Jean gave her one bitch blow that echoed throughout the airport. The thunderous slap silenced everyone. ZNS reported that Jean ordered everyone on the ground and they subsequently complied. *Another version of this story says that Jean was actually in the Atlantis Resort's casino and that it was a guest that he had slapped and held hostage.*

In whatever version of this part of the story you believe, apparently there was a brief standoff. Until the police boom rushed and cut Jean's ass for doing shit, particularly to foreign Americans. Jean was eventually charged with whatever charges they levy on people who do that type of shit.

I remember watching ZNS as Jean was escorted shackled and handcuffed to court. I remember him smiling broad teeth and spitting at the camera. He had a dazed look upon him. At one point as he passed a female reporter with her cameraman, Jean whispered to her in a sultry voice, "Hello Clarise" and then flickered his tongue like the character Hannibal Lecter in the movie *Silence of the Lambs.*

Eventually, Jean was ordered to attend Sandilands Rehabilitation Center to have a psychiatric evaluation done on him. He was released some months later. I saw him once after that; he was talking big talks about getting better, about getting back on track, and accomplishing his dreams. I remember asking him about Pookie and his baby. He said Pookie's family does not allow him to see them. I also asked him if he still does hear the voices...he went silent for a few seconds, but eventually said yes...but they are quieter now.

2 days after my brief conversation with Jean, he was found dead on Cabbage beach, his body stiff and bloated from the water. I sincerely believe the voices had returned and that he could not control the impulses. I want to believe that instead of giving in to their commands, Jean decided to drown them out; and just like the demons that were cast into the pigs by Christ, I believe Jean decided to silence the voices, forever.

PLAY

by Charlene Ann Benoit

"Alex, you should really stop being so loud, your mother has a headache," Margaret said calmly.

"I'm sorry Grandma, I just wanted to play," the five-year-old replied sadly as he placed his little toy firetruck on the coffee table.

"I know Sweetheart. Maybe we could do something quiet together?"

"I don't remember when she felt well. Mommy never wants to play, ever."

"I know, she's been going through a lot."

Alex plopped himself down next to his grandmother who was flipping through television stations, "Is there anything good on?" He asked.

She put her arm around him and smiled, "what would you like to watch?"

"Cartoons. Not the news, it's boring and for old people," he giggled with a deliberate idle twinkle in his eye, then nestled into his grandmother.

"Cartoons are a wonderful idea," she whispered softly as she pulled him closer.

***

After spending most of the afternoon watching television, drawing, listening to stories his grandmother read, and playing with the magnets on the refrigerator door, Alex grew restless and went to rummage through his bedroom closet.

He remembered the day his mother took his crib out of his room and painted the walls a different shade of blue. She had placed a bookshelf in one corner and filled it with hard-covered copies of nursery rhymes, fairy tales, and adventure stories. Sometimes, he would take them all off of the shelves and flip through them just to look at the pictures.

At the foot of his "big boy" bed was a bin filled with the toys she'd bought him. His favourite, however, was a special teddy bear that played the sound of his heartbeat. On days when she seemed especially sad, she would go into his room and hug his bear. The smell of her perfume clung to its nearly pristine fur. He lost count of how many times he hugged that bear, breathed in the smell, and cried wishing that she would hug him that way.

He gave up his search, grabbed a bright red ball from the toy bin, and bounced it down the hall and over the stairs.

Andrea was sitting in the living room, meticulously folding the clothing she had just taken out of the dryer. Margaret sat in an armchair across from her and was talking in the same firm tone she used with Alex whenever he was in trouble. He stopped bouncing the ball, held it in his small hands, sat down, and listened intently to every word his grandmother said.

"You know, that boy loves you Andrea. More than anyone has ever loved you. He and I... we don't need to be here. We could have easily left. I needed to make sure that both of you were going to be okay. Then, well after the incident, you were never the same... so I stayed. I understand exactly what you are going through. What kind of mother would I be if I didn't? But you can't keep going on this path. Do you have any idea what you are doing to him? As much as Kyle and I disliked each other, perhaps he's right, maybe you need to consider seeing a therapist."

Andrea didn't say a word, she paused and then finished folding the shirt she was holding. She tried her best not to break down into tears when she lifted one of Alex's teddy bears from the basket. She stared at it for a moment as though she were under a trance, then, like an overfilled cup, she could no longer contain her tears and started sobbing inconsolably.

Alex stood up and continued bouncing his ball over the remaining steps. When he got to the bottom, he could feel his mother staring at him and the ball, so he dropped it and watched as it rolled across the hardwood floor.

She wiped the tears from her face and put the bear and the clothes back in the basket. As she headed towards the stairs, she eyed the ball, then bent down to pick it up; she'd put it away along with everything else.

Alex just stared as she took his toy away. An odd combination of anger and sorrow coursed through him. His anger quickly dissolved into guilt and his jaw dropped as she walked on a toy car he'd left on the stair. Andrea abruptly slipped and dropped everything she had in the basket.

"You've got to be kidding me. I don't know why I bother with anything anymore. Why do you need to do this to me? I'm sure if there's a god, he hates me. Maybe I deserve this," she said, her voice heavy with defeat. As she looked at the mangled mess, she didn't know whether to cry or scream. She was so incredibly exhausted that she didn't know much of anything anymore. So, she left it all there and went to bed without saying another word.

"Grandma, can you help me pick up all of the things Mommy dropped, please? I know it's my fault. I shouldn't have left my toys on the stairs," he said, his face blotchy from crying. She could tell he was almost ready to cry again.

Margaret's eyes grew soft with overwhelming sympathy for the little boy, "Sure Sweetheart, I'll be more than happy to help you," she replied as she got up out of her chair.

***

The sun was filtering through the kitchen window the following morning. Alex sat next to his mother as she set the table for breakfast. She didn't say a word, but she was biting her lip as though she were thinking hard about something. He couldn't quite figure out what it was that had her so bothered.

"Mommy, can we go outside today? It's really pretty out. Maybe we can go for a walk or something?" He asked. His voice was filled with sadness and insecurity, but yet he still maintained hope that she'd say yes.

He watched as she poured cereal into a bowl and emptied the last of the milk on top of it. She placed a glass of orange juice beside it.

"You need to eat. The lady at the grocery store mentioned how sick you've been looking lately."

"But Mom, I look fine. I didn't even go to the grocery store with you," Alex replied, puzzled.

"You also need to remember to make a list of things that are running low, otherwise you are never going to remember to pick them up. You've been such a scatterbrain lately."

"Mommy, I don't understand what you're talking about. I'm horrible at spelling. I can draw you a grocery list. You can bring it with you when you go out. Maybe next time you could even take me with you?"

He sat there and waited for her to respond, but she just stared at the cereal box on the table.

"Mommy, say something please?"

Still not a word.

"Talk to me, please. What did I say that was so bad?" He asked in frustration as he got up from the table, knocking over the glass of orange juice with his elbow. His eyes widened as he watched it shatter on the floor.

"Seriously, I don't need this today. I honestly don't know how much more of this I can take," she muttered as she got up from her chair. She went to grab a roll of paper towels from the kitchen counter and began cleaning up the mess of orange juice and broken glass.

As she knelt there on her knees crying and cleaning, Alex started sobbing, "I'm sorry Mommy. I didn't mean to." When she didn't look at him or answer, he stormed out of the kitchen and into the backyard, slamming the door hard behind him.

Startled, Andrea jumped and cut her hand open on a shard of broken glass. She sat there for a few moments and wept, her blood amalgamating with the juice she hadn't finished wiping up.

***

Andrea had managed to gather enough courage to drive to the store for milk that afternoon. When she returned, Alex and his grandmother were both sitting on the porch swing, his head on her shoulder as they slowly swung back and forth. She cringed at the squeaking of the metal chains and looked straight through them with a look of exhaustion sprawled all over her face.

For a moment, Margaret thought Alex was going to fall asleep, but she knew that would never happen, so she just held him. A little while later, he asked, "Grandma, what was Mommy like before she got sick?"

Margaret paused for a moment, "Well, your mommy was almost always happy. She loved helping people. When she graduated high school, she decided she wanted to be a nurse, so she went off to university. That's where she met your daddy."

He looked down at his feet and pouted, "I don't really remember Daddy that well. I see his pictures in photo albums when Mommy looks through them. She talks about him and tells me how much she wishes things had been different. Grandma, why did Daddy leave?"

Margaret felt so sad for her grandson, he had been without affection from either of his parents nearly all of his life. "I guess he couldn't bear to keep watching your mom get sicker and sicker. He didn't understand what she was going through, so he felt he had to leave."

Alex looked confused, "But Grandma, when you love someone, don't you stay? He could have stayed with me and Mommy."

"I guess there was a part of him that did what he thought was best. He does call your Mommy from time to time and drops by to check on her."

"I know, but still."

She could hear the frustration in his voice and watched as he got up and started throwing things around the room. When he got to the kitchen, he started slamming the cupboard doors and knocking everything over. She got up from the sofa in an attempt to calm him down, but it was too late; Andrea was now standing in the kitchen holding her head in her hands and screaming, "Stop it, just stop it, please just leave me alone! What the hell is wrong with you? I seriously can't take this anymore. Just go away!"

The small boy stopped what he was doing and ran back to his grandmother with tears streaming down his face, "She doesn't want anything to do with me Grandma, she hates me."

"She doesn't hate you Alex... she just doesn't understand."

***

He sat on his mother's bed and watched as she combed her long brown hair in front of the wrought iron mirror. He thought she was the most beautiful woman that ever existed, though she looked different than she did in pictures of her and his dad. She had lost a lot of weight and there were dark circles around her eyes..

She stopped combing her hair for a moment and looked at Alex's framed baby picture that she kept on her vanity. "I'll always love you, I hope you know that. You will always be my baby," she said as she wiped a few tears from her cheek.

"I know Mommy, I'll always love you too. I just wish you would play with me and do other things... but you barely leave your room," he mumbled as he jumped off of the bed. He ran to hug her, but she got up and walked to her closet.

As she opened the closet door, the phone rang. Alex listened as she answered it and knew that it was his dad.

"Hey, Kyle. Yeah, I am getting ready for the appointment. I promised you I would go, didn't I? I'm just looking for something to wear," she said and then paused as she listened for a moment. "Yes, I will be ready soon. I told you I just need to get dressed. Just ring the doorbell when you get here, or if you still have your key, then you can let yourself in."

She hung up the phone and quickly changed into a plain grey dress. Alex could tell she didn't want to go, but he was happy to see that she was finally willing to see a doctor. Maybe they could help her get better.

***

"I don't think the medication the doctor gave Mommy is helping her any. She sleeps way more than she used to," Alex grumbled.

"I know Sweetie, I'm worried about her too."

"Have you tried talking to her? She won't listen to me and hasn't said anything to me in weeks."

"Trust me when I tell you, she doesn't listen to a thing I say either. She hasn't since she was a teenager," she laughed.

Andrea was sleeping on the sofa this time. He quietly walked over and brushed her hair away from her face. She looked almost peaceful. He put his head to her chest, like he often did, and listened to the beating of her heart. It was slower than it usually was. He hoped she was finally having sweet dreams and not the nightmares that normally awoke her and resulted in her screaming.

Alex decided to watch his favourite cartoon and play with one of his favourite cars while his mother slept. After a few hours, he noticed that she wasn't moving at all anymore, not even to change her position. He went over and gently touched her shoulder, "Mommy? Are you okay?" His grip tightened on her shoulder, "Mommy wake up!"

Overhearing the commotion in the living room, his grandmother came back to see what was going on, "What's wrong?" She asked.

Alex's face was streaming with tears, "Grandma, she won't wake up."

Margaret watched as her grandson kept shaking his mother, a little harder and harder each time. He yelled loudly in her ear and at one point even pried open her eyelids with his little fingers.

He had all but given up when she opened her eyes and looked at both of them with a puzzled expression on her face.

"Mom? What are you doing here?" She asked as her eyes fixated on her son. It took her a moment to acknowledge what was happening. She was still a little incoherent as if she'd just woken up from a really long dream. "Alex?" she asked, her blue eyes brimming with tears.

"It's me, Mommy, are you okay?"

"Yeah Baby, Mommy is going to be okay."

In a matter of seconds, the last five years flooded through her mind. She remembered walking into his nursery and turning on the lamp before tucking him in for the night. She remembered his pink little face turning blue and how he wasn't able to breathe. She remembered screaming for Kyle to call an ambulance while she gave him mouth to mouth on his changing table. She remembered begging and pleading with God while she tried to maintain focus and keep her son alive. She remembered everything.

Then there was Kyle. He just stood there in the doorway looking at them, with his phone in his hand and not a single word to say. It felt like an eternity between when she'd demanded he make the call and when he actually picked up the phone to make it. Then, when the paramedics arrived, he stayed behind while she went to the hospital with their baby. Her baby.

Things didn't get better after that night. She went further and further into her journey of darkness and despair. She felt like a failure and her bitterness towards Kyle had continued to grow. She couldn't help but blame him in some way. It had gotten to the point that he couldn't take it anymore, and on Alex's first birthday, they had a huge fight and she had told him to leave.

So many birthday presents she'd bought that year and every year after. She didn't miss a single one. There wasn't a birthday cake she didn't bake, or a candle she didn't blow out making wishes especially for him.

She thought back on Alex's first Christmas. It had been relatively quiet except for his incessant crying. She still hadn't returned to work and had spent the bulk of her days rocking back and forth with her legs folded on her bed. She wanted to be able to hold him and soothe him and give him all of the love he deserved to have, but she felt lost and so incredibly empty.

She would often hear the faint rocking of the chair in the nursery and the sound of her mother singing lullabies. There was a part of her that felt overwhelmed with jealousy, but that jealousy was fueled by relentless guilt and her belief that she had been a bad mother and wife. She wanted a chance to do everything over from the very beginning, but life is never kind enough to offer do-overs without the fabric being marred by stains.

Now, five years later, it all made sense. She was never crazy; he was never really gone. She thought about all of the times she'd gotten angry and upset over bouncing balls, broken dishes, and toys left on the stairs. He'd been there the whole time.

"I'm so sorry Alex, I didn't know. I..."

"It's okay Mommy. I forgive you. It's all going to be okay, you don't need to cry anymore," he whispered as he hugged her tightly.

It was the first time in five years that she was able to hold him back. The emptiness she had felt for so very long was now gone.

"Mommy?" Alex asked as he pulled away.

"What is it, Baby?"

"Will you play with me now that you're feeling better? Please?"

Andrea glowed and tears ran down her face, "I would be more than happy to play with you."

***

It was nearly ten-thirty when Kyle decided to go check on Andrea. He'd spent the better part of the afternoon and evening trying to call her, but couldn't get an answer. When he arrived at the house, he rang the doorbell and knocked several times before going back to his car to get his spare key in order to let himself in.

The house was eerily silent except for the sound of cartoons playing in the background. He almost tripped over a few toy cars that were lined up in the foyer. He saw Andrea laying on the sofa; her skin was pale and she held an empty pill bottle in her hand. She wasn't breathing and, when he checked, she had no pulse and was as cold as ice.

He was glad it was finally over. He never imagined that it would take five years, and even then he had to take it upon himself to switch out her anti-depressants for sleeping pills. No one would question her overdose, just as no one questioned when his son died from the Fentanyl he had put in his formula so many years before. His friend at the medical examiner's office stated SIDS as the cause of death.

He smirked when he thought about his mother-in-law dying from cardiac arrest. No one ever knew he injected the air into her bloodstream that caused her embolism. SIDS and a heart attack... easily explainable. He was a respected doctor and his wife had been a nurse; there was never enough suspicion from anyone other than Andrea to ever require autopsies. It was her suspicion that drove him to find a subtle, but sure way to get rid of her. Her mind had been broken so badly, he knew it wouldn't take much to push her over the edge. Now, finally, it was finished and he could breathe.

As he dialed 911 for the third time in that house, he wondered if he would move back in or if he would just sell it. He froze for a moment; he couldn't help but noticed the smile on Andrea's face... and felt a shiver run down his spine as though he were being watched.

CLOSURE

by C.N. Greer

She never thought she'd come back here. The gravel crunched beneath her feet as she made her way down the dusty driveway. The breeze was stale in the dry heat and did nothing but move the dark hair momentarily from her back as the sweat dripped down between her shoulder blades. It had been nearly two decades since she'd stepped foot on this property since she'd faced what had happened here. Since she'd faced what she'd lost here. And the only reason she'd come back at all was to see it gone.

Sound didn't exist around that house as it had when she was a teenager, the world slipped away and she, the house, and the ghosts of her past were the only things of substance that mattered right then. It wasn't much of a house then, much less anymore, the structure resembling a dilapidated old shack. Even back then, the paint had been peeling, the deck was rotting, the boards sinking and swayed, bleached gray from the sun. The dry brown grass had grown wild and brushed the bottom of the dingy windows. The inside, she knew, wasn't much better. The wallpaper was ripped in the living room, the bedrooms were in desperate need of repainting. The bathroom pipes were exposed and the back bedroom was nearly unlivable. Yet none of that bothered her.

It was what happened upstairs that made her want to run away.

She'd been sixteen when she met him—young, confident, carefree. Looking back, she hardly recognized herself, but she remembered him. He'd been the coolest guy at the party, the bad boy who stood back from the crowd, surveying the drinking teenagers with an above-it-all attitude. Every guy at the party deferred to him, the girls watched him with interest, yet he stood there surveying the crowd, completely uninterested in anyone around him. Then his eyes landed on her. It didn't take long for the two of them to start dating. He'd pursued her relentlessly while still making it feel like she was the luckiest girl in the world just by receiving his attention. And, like the giddy teenager she was, she believed him.

It hadn't lasted long. Within months, the sweet facade began to fade and the "I love yous" followed by the subtle criticism and guilt trips. He'd tell her he loved her hair while saying she could be skinnier. He'd praise her legs while hinting her breasts could be bigger. He'd tell her how much she meant to him while implying she could do more to prove she cared. "I don't know," he said one night, sitting on the edge of his bed, "I just thought you wanted to spend time with me. But you'd rather go hang out with your friends."

Suppressing a sigh, she shook her head. "That isn't it at all. But I spend all my time with you; I hardly ever see them. Are you really going to tell me that means I don't care?"

"Whatever," he replied, turning away from her. "Do what you want." So, she'd canceled her plans. Her friends could wait, but he wouldn't and she was terrified of what she would be without him—if anything at all. No matter how she tried to please him, it was never enough and anytime she mentioned her feelings, she would end up in tears while he scolded her and told her she didn't love him enough. After a while, she believed him, and the part of her that had been happy, confident, and carefree slowly died.

"Are you lost?" a voice called, jarring her from her thoughts. An old man stood in the field, his dinging white shirt and coveralls blending in with the tall grass.

Was she lost? In more ways than one. "No, I'm not lost," she called back. "Sorry, I hadn't realized anyone was here."

The old man smiled, an unlit cigarette dangling from the side of his wrinkled mouth. He nudged his shoulder toward the house.

"Used to be yours?"

She shook her head. "No, but I used to know someone who lived here."

"Same people for the last forty years," he said. "Think the son owns it now. Shame, really. He let it go to shambles. They're knocking it down next week. Too bad the kid doesn't know how to take care of the things he's got."

"Yeah," she muttered, "too bad."

That night he broke her he'd thrown a party. The house was filled with people; everybody was drinking and having a good time. Everyone, that is, except him. She'd tried to enjoy herself, but his sullen, sulky moods always made that impossible. After a while, he grew bored and managed to convince her to go upstairs. "I just want time alone with you," he said. "To talk. It's so noisy down here." Yet, once he got her alone, he only wanted one thing.

She hadn't wanted to sleep with him. Right then, she didn't even like him. She'd grown so tired of the guilt and the shame, but still, she couldn't leave. She couldn't make herself walk down those stairs. So, she stayed. And they fought. It felt like hours, though it may have been only one. But by the end of it, she was so turned around, so confused as to what they were even fighting about in the first place. He kept insisting if she didn't sleep with him, she didn't love him. Shame, insults, guilt, and declarations of love all mixed together in a cruel bout of emotional warfare. He could have been beating her with his fists and it would have made more sense. She was sixteen years old. All she knew is she wanted the pain to stop.

So, she said yes. And she thought it would stop. But all it did was change form. She'd never seen him move so fast. She stood there while he kissed her, while he undressed her, tears streaming down her face, arms limp at her sides. When he laid her down on the bed, she didn't embrace him. Instead, she laid there on that corner of the bed, crying silently, staring upwards and counting the cracks in the ceiling tiles, waiting for it to be over.

There were thirty-two.

When he finished, he dressed and went downstairs to get himself another drink. Once he was gone, she dressed as quickly as she could, then curled up in a ball on the other side of the bed and cried herself to sleep.

She wished she could say that was the end of it, that the abuse stopped. But it didn't, not the emotional or the sexual. She wished she could say she'd left him after that first time, but she couldn't. It wasn't always bad, she recalled. And she understood now why women stayed with their abusers. No matter how loud her voice was screaming that his poisonous words didn't matter, his voice was louder. Always louder. And for the longest time, it kept her from believing she had any worth. So she stayed because she didn't believe she was good enough to be with anyone else.

The fear had set in then. She was terrified to displease him. But no matter how hard she tried, it was never enough. She was never enough. When it happened a second time, she learned how to hate. This time, when she gave in after fighting the mental battle she knew she would lose, there were no tears. There was no love. She'd gone numb. She didn't need to count the cracks in the ceiling tiles because she knew how many cracks there were. She knew his breath against her skin, his body rutting on tops of hers. She knew it wouldn't last long. She'd been there before. And right then and there, she promised herself she would never be there again. So, she waited. And when he finally got off of her, she left. And still, she didn't cry.

She'd gotten the nerve to break up with him a couple of weeks later. She thought she'd feel free, or at least lighter, but she didn't. At the time, she hadn't understood what those incidents meant, and she blamed herself for everything he'd put her through. She didn't call it rape. She never called it rape. She believed it was her fault. Sometimes, late at night when the world went quiet and all she had were her thoughts, she still believed that.

It wasn't until she was in college that she even admitted anything had happened. The word "rape" didn't even cross her mind. She'd said yes, hadn't she? It was a botched flirtation with her new boyfriend that planted the seed that she'd gone through anything wrong. Until she'd been sobbing uncontrollably after something as innocent as being tickled, she hadn't even considered it.

"What happened to you?" he asked, staring at her in horror.

Pulling her knees up to her chest, she looked away. "Nothing happened to me."

He shook his head. "People don't start crying over nothing. Something happened." Taking her hand, he caressed her skin, gently running his other hand through her hair. She tried not to flinch. It didn't make sense—she knew it didn't—but in that moment she didn't feel safe. She'd never been attacked, never been physically abused, so why was she pulling away from this boy who loved her? Why did she suddenly feel so vulnerable and ashamed? Nothing had happened to her. But in the back of her mind, she knew that was a lie. From that point on, whenever she asked herself that same question, those two nights counting ceiling tiles with tear-stained cheeks came to mind.

Then one day she was sitting in her Human Sexuality class, and the words "Coercive Rape" were written on the board. She wasn't even paying attention to the reading; it had been a rough day and she wasn't in the mood to learn. But she couldn't block out what she was hearing. Words like "manipulation" and "coerced consent" flooded her senses, and as her instructor read the description aloud, anger-filled every fiber of her mind and tears flooded her eyes. Without a word, she'd gathered her things and fled from the room.

It wasn't until a few nights later, half a bottle of vodka gone and ugly words covering the pages of her journal, that she was able to admit what had happened. She'd been raped. No, she hadn't been attacked, but she had been violated. She'd said yes, but what she'd meant was she wanted it to stop. He could have her body if he would quit hurting her mind. Guilt and shame were more effective weapons than fists could ever be. Staring down at the pages of black ink pressed hard into the paper, she ran her fingers over the tear stains blurring her words. Rape. She'd been raped. And all those suicidal thoughts, all the depression and hateful words she'd been so dismayed by all those years finally started to make sense. Something had happened to her—she was a statistic. Now she had to figure out how to move on.

He'd taken so much from her, she thought, staring at the darkened windows of his bedroom. Her innocence, her confidence. Her safety. Even now, years later, he'd taken a part of herself she still didn't know how to get back. Was it any wonder she needed to overfill on whiskey to feel even a little bit safe in bed? Didn't it make sense that she could so easily detach her emotions from the act of love itself? Even when she'd run into him five years before, she'd had a panic attack the moment he'd left. How much more was she going to let him take from her?

Moving over to the shade, she sat down at the base of the tree and watched the man collect old clothes and garbage from the field, smoke from his cigarette swirling around in gray spirals up into the sky. She suspected there would be a fair amount of cleanup even before the demolition.

She didn't hate him. Oh, how she wished she did. But she couldn't hate him—not really. The fact was, she'd never really seen him as the bad guy—not even when she was finally able to put the responsibility for his actions on him. He scared her, yes, but not because she thought he would physically hurt her. More, she was afraid of what she would let him do. He had a way of getting inside her head and twisting her thoughts and she didn't even think he realized he was doing it the majority of the time. For that, she felt sorry for him, she was leery of him, but she didn't hate him.

She hated herself though. For a long time, she blamed herself for giving in to him, for believing him, for letting him break her down so low that he could build her back up the way he'd wanted. Over the years, she'd desperately fought to regain her control. She even thought sleeping with him again on her terms might be the answer, but in the end, it had just left her empty. She'd had to tear apart everything she thought she was, take the control back from him like breaking a bone to set it again.

Until one day she'd finally been able to breathe.

It hadn't been easy. Every step forward had been hard-won. Every time she thought she was making progress, something would bring her back to that bedroom, to those ceiling tiles, and her climb to being healed would start all over again. But she was relentless. No matter what he took from her, how many barbed words he used to slice her confidence, he'd never been able to get through that stubborn streak or her determination. She refused to be a victim. She was more than that, better than that. She needed to know her past would not define her or dictate her present. So, she fought, and little by little she regained all the pieces she'd lost along the way.

When she met the man she called her husband, she'd had to steel herself to tell him the truth. He deserved to know. She'd told people in the past and received responses ranging from "Oh man, that sucks," to "Well, you said yes. Why didn't you tell the police? It wasn't really rape." She had no idea how he would take it, but to her surprise, his eyes filled with sympathy and compassion.

Taking her hand, he kissed her fingers. "I'm so sorry that happened to you," he told her. He brushed a tear from her cheek. "But I promise, nothing like that will ever happen to you again." And he'd meant it. He was kind and gentle, with a quiet strength he was never unwilling to share when hers wavered. They had a little girl now; they were even talking about having another. Was she really going to let this horror from her past dictate her future or how she thought about herself? Was she going to let it taint the relationship she had now or the relationship she had with her daughter? Was she going to let the shell of a house take away the confidence she'd fought and bled for? She needed to let it go and she knew watching the house get demolished wouldn't actually help—as satisfying as it might be.

"Don't stay out here too long now," the old man told her. "It's hotter than hell in this sun."

When she nodded, he smiled his crooked smile and flicked his cigarette butt into the grass, sparks flying over his gnarled knuckles.

She waited until he disappeared down the long drive before she got to her feet and approached the house again. So much pain haunted those walls when in reality it was just a pile of wood, nails, and glass. And yet, all her nightmares had begun in that house. Reaching down, she picked up a rock the size of her fists and let it fly. It hit the siding with a satisfying thunk followed by the final thud as the board fell to the deck. The anger in her stirred and she reached for another rock. This time, she threw it at a window, loving the sound of glass breaking. Elated, she threw more. Stone after stone after stone, she chucked them into the air, half giddy and half-crazed when they struck their target.

Finally, her chest heaving, her hands on her knees, she felt emptied of all the negative thoughts she'd harbored for so long, each and every one of them scattered in pieces on the deck at the very place they'd been born. She'd been raped. And even though she'd said yes, it wasn't her fault. No, her case would never be reported, never be tried, and she was okay with that. But she had finally come to terms with what she was, and that was never a victim. She was a survivor.

A few feet from the house, a small blaze caught in the grass. Smoke curled in the air with the faint scent of nicotine. The old man's cigarette butt must have caught fire. Exhausted, she went back to her shady seat and sat down. It wasn't long before the flames had made a meal of the dry grass and were beginning to lick the sides of the deck.

Leaning back, she settled in. She watched as the fire consumed the bottom floor of the house. Waited until it blazed in the upper window, purifying the wrongs that had been done there. Night had fallen by the time she stood and started walking to her car. She'd call the fire department when she got to her car, she decided. Once there was no chance of those memories being saved. Smoke permeated the air now, and off in the distance, she could hear sirens. Good, someone else had beaten her to it. She only hoped they didn't get there too quick.

It was over. After so many years of feeling that pain like a sliver beneath the skin, she'd finally pulled it out and watched it burn. Taking her key fob from her pocket, she clicked the top button and up the street, her parking lights flashed in the dark, causing her to smile. She would never have to go back there again. The gravel crunched beneath her feet as she made her way down the dusty driveway.

FAILED EXPERIMENT

by C.N. Greer

I couldn't believe it. After all this time, there she was, casually strolling across the street and back into my life. How many years had it been since I'd seen her last? Two? Almost three? And yet, the second I realized it was her, it was like it had been no time at all.

When we'd first met, there was no one like her. She pushed me and challenged me in ways I didn't realize until she was gone; until I pushed her away. She made it seem effortless. We were effortless. And we could have been so much more than we were. If only I hadn't been so damn scared of settling down, of tying myself to one woman, or focusing on anything but my job. So, I left, giving up the possibilities of what we could have been. And just like she'd said I would, I lived to regret it.

Still, I was surprised when she'd agreed to have lunch with me again. Nervous, I adjusted my jacket, situating it over my shoulders so it fell smoothly down my arms. What would she think of me now? I wondered, thanking the waitress and pulling out a chair. Would she look at me the same way? Maybe. Maybe she'd think the years had been as good to me as they had to her.

Impatient, I toyed with the white tablecloth brushing my thighs. There was a thread loose, and I couldn't help but pick at it.

The day was warm, the light breeze making the outside café the perfect venue. There were flower baskets along the iron railing and a vase on every table. Ours was a red so dark it was almost purple. It struck me as a flower she would like. At least I'd have something to look at until she got there. The last thing I needed was for her to think I was preoccupied with my phone.

I didn't have to wait long, however. Within just a few minutes, I heard the click of heels down the sidewalk. Hastily, I wiped my palms on my jeans and stood to greet her.

She looked just as beautiful as I remembered. Her long, auburn hair cascaded around her shoulders in waves and her red sundress billowed around her hips showing just a hint of leg. For a moment, I was lost in time, to another sunny day we spent entirely in bed.

"Hi," I said, my voice slightly cracking. Silently, I cursed my luck.

Her lips twitched and she leaned in for a hug. Man, she even smelled the same.

The waitress returned and took our orders. We chatted about this and that, making small talk until our food came. The longer I sat across from her, the more awkward I felt. Was this the right thing to do? Here we were, eating in relative silence, trying not to let our past get in the way. And yet, that's all it was doing. Every memory of her I'd ever had was sitting there with us, reminding me of all I had lost.

Finally, I couldn't take it anymore. "So, this is weird, right?"

A question furrowed her brow. "What is?"

"This. Us. Me, sitting here having lunch with my ex-girlfriend like it's nothing. It feels weird to me. I mean, doesn't it feel strange to you?"

The look she gave me was a quizzical one. Up until then, she'd been as pleasant as ever, but I swear, thunder rolled through those pretty green eyes.

"Seriously?" she asked, raising one eyebrow. "I am not your ex-girlfriend. I am not your ex-anything. The title of 'ex' requires a relationship, and a relationship requires time. Time, opportunity, the chance to build, to evolve, to grow. Time to see if we could reach the potential that drew us to one another in the first place. We didn't have a relationship. We never got the chance.

"What we had was more like a failed experiment. We had the chemicals right. On paper, they told a story that would be any chemist's dream. But the product didn't pan out. A mole here, an electron there. Apply too much heat—or too little—and one side is affected by the catalyst while the other is not.

"The interesting thing though is to watch it switch. See, all these molecules are just hanging out, content with the world around them. Not looking for a change. But put within proximity of each other, those molecules start to bounce around, to ping off the confines of their comfort zones until the elements collide, creating something entirely new. Each element is still its own, but they're sharing electrons now, and so have created a completely unique molecule.

"In theory." Leaning back, she studied me, daring me to contract her, to interrupt her. I wasn't stupid enough to try.

"Yet, there must have been something wrong with the reactants," she continued. "The equation must not have been balanced. Because when our elements combined, we had heat. We had a reaction. Our molecules collided, fusing to one another with reckless abandon, spurred on by the catalyst which went from one reactant to the other before dissolving enough that the only thing left to do was spontaneously combust.

"So, in the experiment that was us, the product failed. The question now then, is to decide what to do with what's left. Do we try the experiment again? See if we can get it balanced, give it the time it deserves to do so, and become an actual relationship? Or do we simply pour the chemicals down the drain?"

Minutes passed. Days, it felt like. Weeks. I stared at her, waiting for an answer, refusing to accept that the question might have been rhetorical. "Well?" I demanded when she remained silent, anxiety fueling my impatience.

She just watched me, as if weighing her options, carefully crafting her response, silently searching for the right words to get her point across without giving anything away. It was something she was quite good at and silly me, I was only just beginning to see it.

And then she smirked at me. Yes, smirked. That warm, bubbly personality I was used to had cooled to someone I was terrified to understand. She met my gaze with sad eyes and a wry smile, peering at me through the veil of sarcasm she hid behind like a mask to disguise her pain. And if I didn't know her any better, I might have bought her act. I might have believed she didn't care about the answer at all.

"You tell me," she scoffed, the perfect picture of nonchalance. "You're the scientist."

Then she left, and I was all alone with my thoughts. As I watched her walk away, her hair blowing in the wind, I realized she was right. She'd always been right. It was up to me.

The problem was I just didn't know.

A DREAMER OF DREAMS

by Emma Gledhill

She had spent so many minutes, hours, and days in her life daydreaming of it all being different. Daydreaming of riches, of perfect jobs, and even of the existence of magic in some form or another. Before bed each night she would place hope for more inside a wish, which she would send up to the starlit sky above.

Seren was an avid reader. She had been since she was a little girl and although being so had brought her great joy and a very broad vocabulary, it had also given her the most detailed driven, vivid imagination. This was a blessing and a curse as the 'more' she dreamed of, would always be out of her grasp.

As a child she would dream of far off lands, she would draw colourful, detailed pictures of animals and people she'd never seen in life but had glimpsed a mind's image of from books. She had written stories about people and their adventures, always assuming when she was old enough that she would have adventures of her very own. She would often slip off in her mind to places unvisited and times that never were, to then snap back to her, often boring, reality.

Seren was thirty-eight years old and had a job that paid her bills. Everything was just OK. Everything was satisfactory. Everything was average.

She had longed for more but hadn't the courage to take the steps for anything more than what she had. Her job was safe and known to her, on a route she'd travelled for many years. Everything in her life was unchanging.

This was until a grey Thursday in February. Her day had unfolded as it always does, nothing exciting nor unexpected. A boring, if not slightly exasperating, day at work surrounded by the same faces as every day had been before.

Seren had stepped on the bus for her journey home and chosen the seat which would place her away from the majority of the passengers. She wasn't someone who enjoyed human contact, beyond those people that she loved.

With her seat found, she took from her bag the latest book she was engrossed in and began to read. She would escape inside books for as many hours as she could, living the life of the protagonist of each adventure. Her books were her treasures and her doorways to 'more'.

The bus eventually reached her stop and she departed with a thank you and headed towards her lane. The evening light was now in short supply and the streetlights glowed and hummed above.

It was then, looking towards her front door, which she was still a distance away from, that she saw a large envelope hanging from her letterbox. She wasn't too happy to see this, of course, there was data protection to think of! Anybody could have taken it!

As she approached, she was also a little confused. Her life was predictable. All bills arrived at the same time of the month or by electronic mail and it was extremely unusual for her to have a letter arrive, out of the blue.

She got to her door and pulled the envelope from the letterbox. The envelope had only four words written on the front, it was a silverlike, glistening ink that formed the most beautiful handwriting.

The words on the front were 'Seren, Dreamer of Dreams.'

She was baffled. For the life of her, she couldn't imagine who would send her mail other than bills and the title couldn't have been more odd, sat there in the centre of this crisp white envelope. It was her name of course yet strangely after the initial oddness, the title they used settled comfortably on her shoulders.

She put her key in the door and opened it. She locked the door behind her and placed her keys and the envelope on a small table by the door while she took off her coat and shoes and placed her bag on its hook. A routine she undertook daily.

She picked up the ominous envelope and walked to her kitchen and switched the kettle on. She sat down at the large wooden kitchen table and carefully opened the envelope. She took another look at the writing on the front and then looked inside.

It contained just one piece of paper. She carefully pulled this out and realised it wasn't just paper, it was parchment. The parchment contained the same silvery, elongated script as the envelope.

She began to read:

Seren,

We have known of you your entire life.

Vibrations are felt in our world when a person with a noteworthy imagination is born. Although noteworthy doesn't really seem a good enough word to describe what you hold behind those hopeful eyes.

We have watched you and been with you along the way for all of these years and as we had hoped, from the moment you began to collect ideas and form sentences, we knew that we had a candidate in the making.

A candidate for what you may say? A candidate for our Head Librarian.

"Librarian?" Seren said out loud. This seemed to be a very strange way of advertising a job. She had always wanted to be a Librarian and had her name, not with any actual intention, on some websites for Library roles. Of course, predictably, being surrounded by and talking about books all day was the ideal way to spend her days, and to be paid for it seemed a bonus but she'd never really pursued it with any effort.

However to advertise a job in this way and for it to be posted through her door without an address or a stamp was incredibly odd. Maybe it was a children's library? Maybe it was a gimmick? Plenty more maybe's floated around in her brain.

Even then...this didn't make much sense. She read on.

Our library is a special one indeed. It holds all the stories written but never published, dreamed of but never written down or spoken but never taken further. These stories create a well of energy. All the valuable time, dreams, tears, and imagination poured into the stories never told create a certain type of magical energy that requires protection from those who may try to use the energy in ways that would be of detriment to us all.

We will not say more of this here and now. There will be a time for more detail but this time is not now.

These stories need protecting by someone who not only loves and cares about stories but one who has many of their own within the library itself. An extraordinary person who needs the stories as much as they need the person.

We are offering you, Seren Richardson, this opportunity and we are all in hope that you do not refuse.

On the reverse of this letter, you will find instructions to lead you to the entrance of our library. You must follow these instructions on the time and date given and we will allow you a period of six hours in the library so that you may meet us and it and feel the importance of the task to be undertaken. You will then be asked to choose.

Understand that once you choose, there is no going back. If you choose the life of the library, this will be your life until the day you die.

If you choose to walk away, this will never be offered to you again and the memory of the offer will be wiped from your mind.

Please think carefully.

We look forward to meeting you in person.

The Elders of the Library of The Never.

Seren placed the letter on the table and blinked a few extremely slow blinks. She had no idea what to think. It was the 'more' she had always dreamed of but with so much unknown about it, how could she decide? There was no doubt that she would go but the doubt would be whether she could give up her family, her home, the potential of future love?

Who were these people? Were they even people? How big was the library? She had so many questions. They would only be answered by undertaking the task described. She turned over the parchment and displayed before her was a neat diagram of directions, in the same writing, which led to an address on the other side of town. It seemed fairly straightforward to get to. What she found when she got there may not be quite so.

The date and time given was midnight in two days' time. Two days seemed so soon yet so long to wait.

How could she undertake normality for the next two days?

There was only one way to find out.

At that moment, there came a deafening beep of a car horn which seemed as though it was right outside her front door. She walked hurriedly to the door and opened it.

The brightest of lights accompanied the loud elongated beep and she felt in that moment as though her whole body was shaken to its core. Her eyes, which were somehow now closed, opened with a jolt.

Her vision was fuzzy. She looked around. She was still sat on the bus, on the journey home from work! The driver was honking the horn at a car that had made a wrong turn and was sat facing the bus, its headlights gleaming. Her book and bag sat before her on her knee.

She looked around and the dismay settled. She realised, she must have fallen asleep, it had all been just another dream.

The issue on the road clear, the bus set off once more. The curse of such a vivid imagination had gotten her.

The bus stopped and still a little dazed she only realised once people began to get off that this was her stop. She hurriedly grabbed her bag and book and ran for the door of the bus.

She got off, giving thanks and stood in the cold evening air, almost dark, yet lit by the streetlights around her. She felt like she could cry tears of hopelessness.

It was just another evening in her mundane, normal life where she longed for more while nothing, as ever, longed for her.

THE ESCAPE

By Emma Gledhill

She couldn't believe that she'd found him. This man. This human being that just seemed to complete her. It felt as though they were lost puzzle pieces that had found their way back and fit together, just so. They had so much in common yet on the other hand, he was the light to her dark, the positivity her negative mind struggled to grasp. So many of their interests intertwined to be, I don't know, a perfect match?

He'd spent so many years searching and gave up and she had spent so many years wanting to escape from the life she lived.

Eleanor Roberts had been stuck in the same miserable, mismatched, mentally abusive relationship for years and had convinced herself she deserved nothing better. She'd convinced herself nobody else would want her.

Her husband was her biggest mistake. He was cruel. He knew her pain but just caused her more. He thought of only himself. He drank, more and more as the years had passed until the toxicity became all-encompassing. She wished she'd walked the other way the day they had met. She was young, just a schoolgirl and she knew no better. He should have.

He took everything from her. Everything, every penny, every hope and dream. It had been years, stuck in a miserable limbo and he'd made it clear he wouldn't let her leave. He controlled so much of her life but in a way that nobody had realised it was happening.

A day had arrived where it had come to a head, she could go no further. She would end her life or her marriage, although marriage seemed too good a word to describe it. Servitude? Torture? A prison of her own making? She'd need to find the courage either way.

She decided to escape, to end her marriage with the help of her family. After a cry for help and admitting what she'd never chosen to admit before, they came for her while he was out. It seemed too easy at the time, the day itself, and looking back it was now a blur.

She'd left it behind but not entirely. Her ex-husband couldn't let her go peacefully. He had seen her only as a possession. Someone to bring home a wage, to cook, and to do what a wife must, according to him. He still tried to torment her from afar. Phone calls at midnight, text messages, emails, even waiting outside her office.

It didn't matter though. He made it bearable. He made it worth the chaos. She could cope with it all if he was by her side.

He. He had a name. His name was Glenn. She had met him just a few weeks after leaving her husband. He'd experienced his own share of torture. His own years of sadness but he was strong enough to have made it part of him. To use it in a way that the past never pulled him down. He had a caring, nurturing way about him and he had made her feel as though nothing could get to her.

He made her smile, even on the days she had forgotten she was capable of it. She saw a future in his eyes. An equal future, with a man she just knew she could trust. With a man who she knew would never hurt her, in any of the ways you can hurt another person.

From that first moment, they never spent a night apart. They grew to know each other as no one had before. They grew to know each other, body, mind, and soul.

Eleanor allowed her brain to make plans. Not for a moment did it feel wrong or too soon. She thought of all the things you should think of in a healthy relationship. Could she marry again? Could she begin to think about children, something that was never an option before? It felt like she could. It felt like she could live and no longer just simply exist.

A few months passed. Those months were filled with happiness. Getting to know another, so deeply, so assuredly. It was love. Storybook love, of what she'd always dreamed.

Today was a day, very much like the others had been, together in their blissful bubble. Eleanor had left work on the usual journey home. Thinking all the way, of seeing Glenn, embracing him and deciding what they would do with their night and their weekend to come. Her life felt so light and free. It didn't matter what their plans were, as long as they were together, she was happy.

She'd gotten home and from the street, she could see all was dark, in her apartment they now shared. Her negative brain went straight to the worst-case scenario. Had her husband truly not given up? Was he waiting, in the dark? Glenn wasn't due to be home yet but they always left the lamps on, always. He knew her fear of the dark, not a fantastical fear of ghosts and demons but of who could be waiting for her. He wouldn't have turned them off. He knew how it would paralyse her.

She couldn't just walk in. She dialed Glenn's number. He answered immediately, just hearing his voice gave her strength. He told her that he'd left all the lamps on as usual. He would never think of turning them out. He knew all too well how the dark made her feel.

He should only be forty-five minutes if she wanted to wait for him but she felt like she needed to be stronger. It'd been weeks without any problems or contact from her ex-husband. Surely he'd given up by now. He had nothing to gain. He wasn't enough of a man to do anything that would involve contact with Glenn.

Maybe it was just a blown fuse. It'd tripped the lights? She told him she'd be fine. He told her she was stronger than she knew and that he loved her. Hanging up the phone, she entered the outer door, making her way up the stairs to the door of her apartment.

Nothing looked out of place, everything seemed as expected. She opened the door to where the switches were and indeed one was up. She switched it and a flash, a shock threw her back.

She was yet to open her eyes, scared of the damage she may have done to herself from the shock. She could hear beeping. Maybe that was a sign that everything was back on? Was it her alarm? The cooker?

She felt a movement by her side, a rustle. Everything was still blurry. Why did it feel like she was unable to move her arms? Wait...or her legs? She couldn't seem to move any part of her body.

She slowly, tentatively opened her eyes. Or did she, it didn't feel like anything moved. Her vision was blurred and it took a moment to clear.

What she could see didn't register at first. She was in some sort of hospital room. The beeping of the machines distracted her from the other noises around her.

A man with his back to her moved into her vision.

"Glenn? Glenn, is that you?"

She thought she'd said it aloud but she hadn't felt her lips move.

A few moments later, he turned around. It was him! It was Glenn! He was here but why was he dressed that way, he didn't look right. He turned to talk to another figure who had entered her line of vision.

No, it couldn't be! What was happening? Why was her ex-husband here? Why was Glenn talking to him.? Why was nobody listening to her cries of fear and frustration?

"Mr. Roberts...I believe that the brain damage your wife sustained during her suicide attempt has led to the state you see before you. As you know, this hasn't improved over the few weeks since she was admitted after the attempt to drown herself in the bath. Her body itself is functioning however her brain is in a state where she cannot talk, communicate or register emotion. She can't hear you. If we gave the authorisation to allow her to be cared for at home, she would need constant care, 24 hours a day and she will never recover. There is nothing further that can be done here to improve her state."

Eleanor silently screamed, without moving a muscle. What!? I'm here. I can hear you! Please don't let him take me home. How can this be happening? Her lips, her tongue...nothing moved.

Her husband glanced at her and smiled, a smile that didn't reach his eyes.

"Thank you Dr Crawshaw, sorry I apologise, you said to call you Glenn. I will take her home and care for her, as long as needed. She is my wife after all."

It was then she realised, like a lightning bolt. That day, she had chosen escape from her marriage but not the way she had just imagined and now this truly was a prison of her own making.

THE GIFT IN THE BOX FILLED WITH LOSS

by Jana Begovic

Going through their mother's belongings felt like an act of bravery. Her wardrobe smelled of honeysuckle soap, and the discreet fragrance seeped into the holes in their hearts, into every tear and laceration mercilessly made by death when it suddenly burst through the doors of their happy life to claim their mother.

Agnes was only sixty years old when she crumpled on the kitchen floor, pulling with her a big red crystal bowl brimming with punch she had just made for her younger daughter's birthday party. The death certificate stated it was a heart attack that cut her life short, and plunged the whole family into an abyss of suffocating grief and disbelief.

Six months had passed before Ann and Beth mustered the courage to open their mother's wardrobe and decide which items to keep and which to donate to charity. Their father did not want to stay home that Saturday and face anew the achingly fresh and unbearable emptiness his wife had left behind. He could not stand looking at the clothes she would never wear again, pearl necklaces that no longer would adorn her slender neck, and shawls the embrace of which her shoulders would not know. His daughters understood his pain and inability to touch his late wife's possessions. He just said, "Do as you see fit."

Gingerly, they caressed their mother's silk blouses, tweed skirts and jackets, black pants and little black dresses, evening and nightgowns, costume and real jewelry, not being able to decide what to donate and what to keep. They sobbed and wept, and then laughed as joyous memories fell out of the boxes filled with photographs, old and faded postcards, and charcoal sketches of nature and animals their mother drew as a hobby.

Rummaging on the top shelf of the wardrobe, Ann, the younger sister exclaimed, "I've just touched something metal, but I can't reach it."

"Let me try," said Beth, a tall and willowy red-haired beauty.

Ann got off a two-step ladder letting Beth climb it and extend her arm across the shelf.

"Is this it?" asked Beth bringing down a yellow tin box with an etching of a blue butterfly on it.

They placed the box on the floor and opened it. A small leather-bound book was in it. The first page had their mother's initials and a crumbling pressed flower that could have been a daffodil once upon a time.

Flipping through the pages, it became clear to them they were looking at their mother's diary, written in neat black cursive. They forgot about the clothes and began to read losing all track of time. Each word led them to a secret world, uncovering facets of their mother's life they had not known, and transporting them to the time their mother lived in Scotland.

In their mind's eye, they could see the verdant rolling hills with grazing sheep, the haunted castles redolent of mysteries, they could feel the insouciance of a young girl in love with nature, a girl with her head swirling with dreams of becoming a ballet dancer one day, and moving to London. With their spiritual eye, they followed their mother to her first dance and smiled reading about her first kiss and her swooning in love with a young man, who had come from England to visit his uncle.

Beth stopped reading when she felt her legs go numb from sitting on the floor. She stood up and lay on her parents' bed, and Ann joined her prodding her to continue reading. "I wonder why mom never told us much about her life in Scotland. And she only went back once to bury her parents," mused Ann.

"I remember her saying she felt no attachment to her home country, and she had no one left there after our grandparents were killed in that horrific car accident. How sad we never had a chance to meet them," said Beth wistfully.

Beth continued to read aloud until she stopped with a gasp.

"Mom got pregnant!"

"What?" asked Ann startled.

The next few entries described their mother's horror at discovering she was carrying a baby at the age of seventeen. The young man she had fallen in love with left her town a few days after he had seduced her. She did not know how to find him because he left without even saying goodbye. She felt too ashamed to ask his uncle to give her his address, because even if he did, what would she do with it? Go to London, knock on his door and tell him she was with a baby? And it has already been four months since he left. Perhaps, he no longer even remembered her.

She confided her secret in her mother expecting she would be disowned, banished, beaten, but her gentle mother, who had always looked frail and irresolute, suddenly turned into a problem-solver asking her daughter to swear to secrecy, and never ever mention to anyone what happened. Agnes nodded in silent acquiescence and shame.

Beth stopped reading and stared at Ann in speechless shock. Ann shook Beth's shoulders and tried to pry the diary from her hands because she could not wait to hear what happened next, but Beth held on to the book firmly, and just whispered, "Wait...I just need a glass of water and a few minutes to process this."

Beth went to the kitchen carrying the diary with her. Ann followed her, and after drinking some water, they both sat at the kitchen table where Beth continued reading the entries aloud.

Their grandmother had a perfect solution. As she had already promised her daughter she would enroll her in a ballet school in London, she talked to Agnes' father convincing him to let her use Agnes' inheritance from her grandparents and send her to London to pursue her ballet dancing dreams. Even though Agnes' father, who was a doctor, was against any artistic pursuits outside of mere hobbies, he agreed, hoping Agnes would soon grow out of that childlike dream, and enroll in medical school following in his footsteps.

Agnes' mother found her accommodations with a distant, widowed cousin who was happy to take a troubled girl in, and the situation also helped alleviate her own loneliness with some company. A private tutor was hired to school Agnes so she would not fall behind in her studies. Agnes was instructed to wear wide-fitting clothing so the tutor would not notice her pregnancy.

Her life began to resemble a surreal story through which she walked like an unwilling character. She went through the motions of daily routine, confused and lost. She felt she was living out a pre-ordained fate, and she resigned to it in powerless surrender. She knew her mother had already found a childless couple who agreed to adopt her baby in secrecy, and not even divulge to anyone that the child was not their own. Her mother told her how desperate for a baby the couple was, especially the woman, who began to wear padding under her clothes and announced to her family and friends she was pregnant.

Agnes had difficulty learning her lessons or concentrating on anything. She felt nauseated most of the time, and achingly nostalgic for her hometown and friends. Every letter from her friends and father gave her fast fleeting joy and she craved more of them. She also felt burning compunction for lying to her father about her ballet lessons, and the progress she had made. One lie tended to turn into an avalanche of falsehoods, she realized with remorse and sadness.

As her belly grew, she stayed more and more confined to the house and her only outings consisted of sitting in the garden and reading. She still daydreamed about becoming a ballet dancer and her mother promised to enroll her in ballet school as soon as she has recovered from birthing the baby. It was to be a gift for her silence about the birth. Her mother explained it was of utmost importance not to bring shame to the family, and especially to her father's booming medical practice.

Her mother spent hours preparing her for the birth and coaching her, especially on how to be completely silent and withstand excruciating pain, for no one must hear her screams. The couple who would adopt the baby had hired a well-known midwife from Ireland and paid her handsomely for her travel, services, and silence. They did not dare hire anyone from London lest their secret be revealed. They paid visits to Agnes bringing her gifts of sweets, books, dainty jewelry, and even pretty dresses. The gifts elicited wan smiles from Agnes, who still felt as if her life were a bad dream from which she would wake up any minute.

The day came when she went into labour. Her mother had arrived two days before and prepared a room in the basement for her. Even if she screamed in pain, the thick walls would muffle the sounds of her agony.

The midwife was highly skillful and her nature exuded confidence. Her instructions were calm and clear and Agnes followed them panting and pushing, pushing and panting, and praying for the pain and torture to end. She whimpered, but never screamed, firm in her resolve to stay brave. She lost all track of time and felt exhaustion overcome her. She pushed once more certain she could never find another ounce of strength to expel the baby from her body, when she heard a cry. She propped herself in bed trying to see the baby but the midwife had already taken it out of the room.

"Where is the baby? Is it a boy or a girl?" croaked Agnes with a voice raspy from exertion.

"It's a girl," her mother replied. "Relax now. The baby will be well-taken care of. You can begin a new life now."

But the new life began with depression. Agnes' body healed but her soul sank into darkness. She felt as if a physical part of her had been severed off violently as if one of her limbs had been amputated. When her mother came again to visit her, she was alarmed by Agnes' listlessness and pallor.

She packed her belongings and took her back home in hope that fresh springtime air and the familiar surroundings would coax Agnes' spirit out of its penumbral hiding, and little by little Agnes seemed to heal, but she was changed. Her carefree spirit was replaced with an air of seriousness laced with melancholy. She no longer talked about becoming a ballet dancer, but to the great satisfaction of her father, readily agreed to enroll in the school of medicine in Edinburgh.

"Mom was such a good doctor, wasn't she?" said Beth and began crying again.

"She sure was. Whenever I was sick, I just knew she would make me feel better in no time. Even her embrace seemed to have healing powers."

"Let's read more," said Beth choking on tears.

Agnes studied with a furious devotion, never missing a lecture, never flinching from autopsies or gagging from the vile smells that sometimes escaped the corpses under her knife. She was filled with a new purpose. She wanted to feel useful and helpful, and once she graduated, she planned to spend a few months working with doctors without borders in Africa.

All her plans came to fruition. She graduated with honours, was offered a job in a small clinic but negotiated with the owner to allow her to start six months later, for she first wanted to volunteer in Zambia.

"Remember mom's stories about Zambia," asked Beth. "She said the experiences were more enriching than she could have ever imagined in spite of the horrible conditions, poverty, and misery."

"Yes, what she found most gratifying was the realization that she was able to make a difference in the lives of so many by using her knowledge and skills," said Ann and continued. "And she met dad there and moved to Montreal. Remember she told us that soon after they left Zambia she heard her parents were killed in a car accident. I wonder if she felt guilty for not having gone back to Scotland to visit them before moving to Canada. I also wonder what happened to their house."

Beth continued to read about her mother's life in Zambia and her falling in love with their dad, the head doctor at the clinic where she volunteered. She soon came to the part in which her mother expressed her devastation over her parents' deaths a few months after she had settled in Montreal. A distant relative was the executor of their will and he arranged for their funeral. That was the last time their mother visited Scotland to say goodbye to her parents at the local cemetery. The house was sold fast and as the only heir, she inherited the proceeds, as well as her parents' savings. She invested the entire sum into a house in Montreal, in which she and her husband raised their two daughters.

They stopped reading the diary because the pain over their loss rippled through their hearts with a renewed force. Just as Beth closed the diary, she noticed an envelope sticking between the last few pages. She pulled it out and opened it. An email printout was in it, as well as a photograph.

"A photo of our mom when she was young!" exclaimed Beth showing the photo to Ann.

"I've never seen this photo of her before. Strange that she's wearing a red dress. She never liked that colour. When was this taken? Her hair is long, and we've only known her with a pixie cut."

Beth did not reply engrossed in reading the email. She was as pale as a ghost when she handed it to Ann.

"What? Tell me? You're scaring me!"

"Look at the date of this email. It is dated one day before our mom had a heart attack."

The email addressed to their mom was written by a woman named Elodie, who was expressing unbridled joy and delight over having found her biological mother, whom she would meet in Canada in the near future.

Beth and Ann looked at each other with eyes wide open.

"Elodie is our sister...she found our mom?" Beth said in a voice brittle with incredulity. "Is all of this just a dream?"

"Let's read the email to the end", cried Ann.

Elodie was writing about her life, her successful career as a veterinarian, and her regret of divorcing her husband and never wanting to have children. She now felt lonely for family and could not wait to meet her biological mother and her half-sisters.

"Mom's reply is here," said Beth excitedly.

In her response, their mom asked her newly discovered daughter for forgiveness for never having attempted to find her, because she was keeping the promise of secrecy to her own mother. She had always prayed for her lost child, never stopping to send her love wherever she was. The trauma of the loss had haunted her through frequent nightmares, and through fear of losing Ann and Beth, but she kept those fears well hidden from her family. After the initial shock of receiving the first email from her lost daughter, she began to feel excitement over meeting her and introducing her to her family. Before she married her husband, she had told him of what happened to her at the age of seventeen, and he showed nothing but understanding. They had a silent agreement that their own children need not know about it. Soon, she would disclose the secret to them, and she had no doubt that her gold-hearted daughters would welcome Elodie with open arms.

"Perhaps, she was planning to tell us about our sister on the day of your birthday," said Beth. "Perhaps, the excitement and the apprehension over telling us caused her heart attack," Beth continued while the sudden tremor in her hands made her drop the paper on the floor. She bent down to pick it up and staggered feeling light-headed from the shock of revelations.

"We have to write to her," cried Ann. I want to meet our sister. She looks like a younger version of our mom. Maybe we can go to Scotland and meet her instead of her coming here? Let's propose that to her."

Beth brought her laptop to the table, went into her email account, and typed in Elodie's address.

"How do we begin? What do we say? This is all so sudden that my head is spinning."

"Just tell her everything, about our mom's diary, the picture and the email we found…tell her we want to jump on the first flight and meet her," said Ann.

"No, we can't say all of that at once…it has to be gradual," replied Beth and began to type.

It took them more than half an hour to compose the email. When they pressed the send button, they looked at each other in disbelief. They poured themselves a glass of brandy and sat in silence. They almost jumped when the reply came soon after. Elodie's words exuded warmth and affection, and a fervent desire to meet them.

Trying to process the sudden happenings, Beth and Ann waited for a couple of days before they wrote again to Elodie. In their email, they told her their dad was happy to learn they found

Elodie, and there were no more skeletons in the family closet left to uncover. They wrote about their childhood, travels, and interests, their careers as a budding fashion designer, and an architect. They sent Elodie photos of their family home, their own apartments, their pets, and even their boyfriends.

Elodie wrote about herself, her happy childhood in England, and how she found out only a year ago she had been adopted. After her initial shock had waned, she began her search for her biological mother. It was Elodie's father who assisted her in getting in touch with one of Agnes' distant cousins, who told her he believed Agnes lived in Canada. Elodie said that she and Agnes had exchanged a few emails since she first established contact with her, and Elodie was all aflutter with joy over the prospect of meeting her mother and her family. When six months ago she saw the obituary online, after she had not heard from Agnes for a few weeks, she was devastated to realize she would never meet her mother. She vacillated about contacting Beth and Ann afraid to add more shock to their grief with her revelation that they shared the same mother.

Beth and Ann continued exchanging emails with Elodie for about four months before they invited her to visit them in Montreal. Elodie replied with a counter invitation proposing they visit her in Aberdeen first. She said she would take the first two weeks of June off work so that she could show them the most beautiful parts of Scotland. Beth and Ann readily agreed.

It took them only a day to sort out their vacation plans at work and find flights. They had never felt as thrilled about a trip as they were now, and their excitement showed in their trembling hands while they were trying to pack their suitcases. In a separate bag, they packed some of their mother's newer clothes, scarves and artwork to offer to Elodie. They also split their mother's jewelry into three parts of similar value and put Elodie's share into a velvet pouch. At the moment they closed their suitcases, a waft of honeysuckle spread through the air.

"Did you smell that?" exclaimed Beth looking at Ann with eyes glistening with tears.

"Honeysuckle," whispered Ann. "Is our mom's spirit around, or did the scent come out of her clothes?"

"I'd like to think it is a sign from her telling us we did the right thing by sharing her possessions with our sister," Beth replied.

The day came when they boarded the Aer Lingus flight to Aberdeen connecting through Dublin. Excitement over meeting Elodie the next day prevented them from falling asleep even for a few minutes. When the plane landed in Dublin, exhaustion and slumber overcame them at the gate causing them to almost miss their connection.

When at last they landed in Aberdeen, Beth and Ann just looked at each other with eyes welling up with happy apprehension they would soon meet the woman who was as much a part of their mother as they were. In silence, they disembarked and walked to the baggage collection area. While waiting for their bags to come, they received a text message from Elodie letting them know she was waiting for them at the arrivals zone.

Once they stepped into the arrivals area, they felt somewhat disoriented by the sight of the crowd waiting for passengers. And then Beth spotted Elodie waving at them and gasped in shock because Elodie looked like a young replica of their mother. She had even cut her hair short. Her embrace was firm and warm, and she smelled of honeysuckle soap. With a voice brimming with joy, she called them sisters and kissed them both on the cheeks. Her embrace felt like a touch of home, like something warm and familiar they had lost and rediscovered. It felt as if life had given them a box full of loss underneath which a most precious of gifts lay —the gift of a sister.

LOST HAPPY

by Jennifer Anderson

I had been enjoying a nice, leisurely stroll through the busiest section of my neighborhood, where everything seemed to take place all at once, the hub, the center. Constant hustle and bustle, people scurrying this way and that. Energy levels seemed to crackle with electricity, the currents almost palpable. I walk amongst this chaos at least once a day; amazed it can take place in such a small area. This nerve center of the neighborhood is probably only a total area of 5 square city blocks, but boy it sure has a ton of activity crammed into it. I am fascinated by the buskers, the vendors shouting out their wares, the carts full of fresh produce, the street performers, and even those who some would call the undesirables. On this particular evening I had been taking in all the sights and sounds when a fluorescent pink heart-shaped piece of poster board, taped to a lamppost, caught my eye.

"LOST," The ad all but screamed at me, as the word had been printed in big, bold, black, block letters. I had to stop and read the rest, curiosity getting the better of me.

Standing with my hands in my pockets I read, "LOST ... one sense of happy. If you know how or where I might find it, please call Guinevere." I had to admit I was intrigued. I also admit to a wee chuckle, lost happy indeed. Who hasn't lost their happy at one time or another? I took note of the number listed; I was going to call Guinevere; I wanted to know who would post such a lost ad. How deep into the depths of despair was this person to reach out in this manner?

I carried on with my walk, fully intending to follow my usual path snaking me through all the nooks and crannies that were hidden amongst the old brownstones in the neighborhood. However, I was not finding the pleasure in the colors, tastes, and sounds that I normally did. No, Guinevere seemed to have taken precedence in my mind. I decided to hurry home and call the number.

As I dialed, I pictured Guinevere in my mind's eye. She would be quiet, timid even. Yes, and young, certainly she was young. Perhaps with a mane of curly blonde locks, softly framing her heart-shaped face, with its china doll like features. Oh, and her eyes would be the color of seafoam, and deep with emotion and feeling. Her cheeks would dimple with her smile and...

"Hello?" A rough-edged husky voice ripped me away from my imaginings.

"Uhh, h-hello," I stammered, certain that I had dialed incorrectly. This certainly wasn't the maiden in distress that I had envisioned; this was some pack a day smoking, whiskey-swilling hag. Thoughts of just hanging up crossed my mind, but I thought better of it and asked, "May I speak with Guinevere please?"

"You've got her," the raspy voice informed me.

"Oh, well then, I've read your ad you see and thought I might be of assistance. I lost my happy once too, and...well, it was quite a journey to finding it again. I would like to help you if I could." As the words came out of my mouth I wondered if I knew what I was doing. Surely this rough-sounding creature on the other end of the phone had brought whatever crisis she was experiencing upon herself. Did she deserve to be aided, or was she meant to be unhappy? I wasn't sure this was my judgment to make, so I waited for her reply.

She seemed to pause before answering and when she did, I was surprised to hear an almost childlike quality to her voice, still raspy but the hard edge was gone. It seemed to tremble slightly as she said, "I would like the help. I just don't know where to look anymore. I've tried everything, I've searched everywhere, and my life still sucks. I'm still unhappy, I'm still bitter and NOTHING goes right or the way I want it to."

I smiled as I suggested a meeting spot, "Do you know where Tasia's Tea House is?"

I heard Guinevere gasp, "I-I go there all the time."

I could hear the suspicion in her voice when she'd regained her composure, "Who are you…really? I mean I've had the stupid ad up for months and no one called. Suddenly today you call and suggest my favorite teahouse as a place to meet. So, who are you?"

I paused for a moment before answering her question, "My name is Pseudo…my parents had a weird sense of humor. I can understand your suspicion but trust me; I can help you. How about if we meet at around three? It's the busy time at the teahouse, so there will be plenty of people around"

Guinevere only hesitated for a second before she slowly answered me, "Yeah, I suppose that would be safe enough. How will I know you? "

I told her that I would know her, after all, how hard would it be to spot someone who had lost her happy. We left it at that; we would meet the next day.

It was five of three when I strolled through the doors of Tasia's. I inhaled the aromas of fresh baked goodies and the sweet and spicy smell of the assorted teas. I loved coming here, and not just for the food and beverage. Tasia's was a myriad of people, styles, and colors. For a people watcher such as myself, it was pure heaven. I came here daily, sometimes even twice in one day depending on the available sights.

Tasia's wasn't just any teahouse; it probably wasn't even what most people would imagine a teahouse to be. Tasia, the proprietress had bought a ranch-style house on the outskirts of town and remodeled it to suit her vision. She wasn't what one would envision the owner of a teahouse to be. Tasia was a throwback to the sixties, maybe even to the era of the gypsy. She wore flowing skirts and billowing peasant blouses in bright colors. Numerous bangles adorned each wrist that would send out chiming tinkles with her every movement. She wore her mane of black hair in a haphazard bun on most days, tendrils of the unruly curls would spring free throughout the day, giving Tasia a carefree, not a worry in the world appearance. She had the skin of a youth, and her cheeks were always rosy. Her eyes glistened with mischief and her laughter spewed forth effortlessly. Tasia truly loved her little piece of heaven on earth. She had worked hard to turn her teahouse into the sought-after artists' hangout that it was.

Great care had been taken in the décor, yet it looked like a mish-mash of retro souvenir explosion. It was filled with bistro-style tables, whose glass-covered tabletops highlighted local artist's work. The seats of the chairs were multi-colored Naugahyde. Overstuffed couches inhabited the areas closest to the dimly lit stage set in the front corner of the teahouse. Beanbag chairs were scattered throughout the place. Burning incense combined with the soft music that played in the background, and strategically placed wind chimes took you back to a freer time the moment you crossed the threshold. Crystals and running fountains could be found throughout the place, also dead center was a fishpond, Tasia loved the relaxing feel these items brought to her place. Handwoven baskets displayed the wares that were made onsite. Smaller baskets adorned the tables holding various condiments and napkins. Funky hanging beads camouflaged the back hall leading to the restrooms. The walls held artwork and framed copies of poetry written by patrons, past and present. Tasia took great pains to ensure her people were well looked after; she knew where her bread and butter came from. Every Wednesday evening was open mike night on stage. Poets, singers, musicians...whatever the genre one could be heard, however, due to the night's popularity one had to sign up for a spot months in advance. All in all, Tasia's had a very "go with the flow" feel to it. It was a place in which all were accepted and encouraged. Tasia's was very much the place to be for anyone who was anyone in the art world.

I chose a table near the back, away from the buzz of the crowd. I wanted to be able to converse with Guinevere without having to speak loudly. I waved the waitress off; I'd wait for Guinevere to arrive.

I sat back and watched the door. I smirked as a gaggle of teen girls came in wearing their skinny jeans, layered shirts, skate shoes, and their multi-colored hair. Several of them had at least one facial piercing and damn near every one of them had her eyes glued to her cell phone screen, thumbs flying over the keypad, text messaging god knows whom. She came in behind these girls.

I knew it was her right away. The funny thing is she could have been any one of those girls if it were not for her age; at least she appeared older than they did. Her face seemed to have a hardness to it, hardness one would find lacking in youth. Her hair was cut short and spiked, it had been bleached blonde with the tips died all different colors. She wore low-rise jeans, and I could see a tattoo peeking out from her right hip as she thrust it out. Her t-shirt was snug and barely skimmed the top of her pants; she wore a brightly patterned sweater over top. Her nose was pierced; she wore very little makeup, a bit of mascara, and lipstick that was too red for her complexion. If not for the tired way she carried herself, her shoulders almost hunched up to her ears, slouched forward as though she carried the weight of the world on her back, her attire and personal grooming would have suggested she was young and carefree. She certainly appeared to be a woman of contradictions. She had a frown line a mile deep in the middle of her forehead and her eyes seemed devoid of emotion as she looked around the teahouse. She stood there, just looking, her mouth turned down as she scanned the patrons.

I stood up and caught her eye. When she glanced my way, I waved her over with a smile. She responded by hitching up the huge bag she called a purse and strode over to where I sat.

I shook her hand and introduced myself, "See, I told you I'd know who you were. I'm Pseudo, it sure is nice to meet you."

We ordered our tea, each of us surprised to find we both favored ginger peppermint tea with lemongrass. We sat in silence, sizing each other up while we waited for our order.

Her grin was lopsided and not quite reaching her eyes as she looked across the table at me. "How'd you know it was me," she asked softly. I could see the distrust in her look; she was hesitant, almost wary as she asked the question.

"You carry the weight of the entire world with you, and it only takes one glance to notice that you have lost your happy." I said with a sad, knowing smile.

"Oh," Guinevere sighed deeply as she slouched down in her chair, her body seemingly liquefying and becoming one with the chair.

Once our tea had arrived, I made a big show of checking on the progress of the steeping. Then I looked across the table at Guinie, as I'd come to think of her. She stared back momentarily and then quickly lowered her eyes. I found myself captivated by the depths of her green eyes, for the life of me I was unable to come up with a name to match the color I saw there.

"So Guinie, where do you think you lost your happy? Can you remember the last time you saw it?" I queried. I hoped she wouldn't mind my using a shortened version of her name; she simply struck me as a "Guinie". I hadn't meant to take such a liberty, however now that I had I awaited her reaction.

Gunevere took a deep breath as she twisted the napkin she held tightly in her hands, "Guinie…wow, I haven't heard that in years. My Grandpapa used to call me that. He passed on 'bout seven years ago, I miss him so much."

I felt bad, "I'm sorry, you just … well, you struck me as a Guinie. It fit so I used it. I won't call you that anymore if you don't like it."

She smiled, and as she did so I could see she was remembering her Grandpapa with fondness. "No, it's alright, it reminds me of him…he was a happy time so it's good." I could see her mentally step back to those happy times. I watched her face soften, if only for a moment and her eyes briefly shone with happiness.

"So, there's a happy memory, is that the last time you saw your happy?" I prompted her, wanted an answer to my question.

Guinie took a deep breath before she continued, "I'm not sure. Right now, I don't remember ever being truly happy. What does true happiness even look like I wonder? I'm not sure I would know it if I encountered it."

I could see her formulating her response as she stirred her tea absentmindedly as she thought for a moment. I sat quietly waiting for her to continue.

"Everything in my life seems to have brought sadness. My Mom's illness and subsequent death when I was a child; my Dad's drinking; my disappointing relationships; my inability to hold a job for any length of time. I just feel like I can't cope some days. Sometimes…" She stopped herself as she took a sip of her tea.

As I listened to Guinie talk, it occurred to me that she was indeed a bundle of contradiction. She appeared to be a rebellious punk with the way she dressed, yet she carried herself like the world had beaten her down. Now, she was speaking with intelligence and great inner reflection. There was definitely more to this girl than my first impression would have indicated, and I found myself intrigued.

"Sometimes what?" I wanted to know.

"Well, sometimes I wish to not wake up. The thought of facing another cookie-cutter day in all its lackluster glory fails to excite me. I'm tired of the sameness. I can't find a way out of this rut."

I looked at her for a long moment before I asked what I wanted to know, "Do you have faith Guinie? Do you have somewhere to turn when the going gets to be too much to deal with all on your own?"

She peered at me over the edge of her cup and replied, "I'm not sure that I have faith in the sense that you are asking. I'm not so sure I believe in God anymore; I mean I know there's something and I do believe in that. I am spiritual, but as for praying, no I haven't done that in a while. I've stopped believing that there is anyone who hears or cares." As she finished speaking, she bit her trembling lower lip to maintain control. I could see the sheen of unshed tears in her eyes.

I held her hand in mine as I gave her the speech, the one I'd heard so many times before. The one that I'd heard given by others when someone was feeling as though the world was against them. The one that my friends had given me in the past, the same one that I, on occasion had chose to ignore. I only hoped that it would get through to Guinie and have an impact on her.

"Guinie, the answer for happiness lies within you. You cannot find it within someone else. You cannot find it within an activity. You must find it within yourself. Take pleasure in who you are and what you do. Embrace yourself, your uniqueness. Worry not about things that have come and gone. Each experience in our lives carries with it a lesson that is imparted to us. If we fail to learn the lesson, we are doomed to the same lesson over and over. What lesson are you failing to get past? Look at all your experiences; what have they been trying to tell you? What have you been ignoring? Delve deep within yourself and you will find the answers...delve deeply and you will know me."

"Oh, and Guinie, find your faith, whatever it may be. We all need to believe in something. We all need somewhere to turn when it seems like the entire world has forsaken us."

I could see the tears in her eyes as she gazed at me. I gently kissed the back of her hand as I got up from the table. I paid for our tab and walked out of Tasia's. I wouldn't return for nearly two years. Guinie would need that time to heal and find herself.

It so happened that there was a poetry reading the day I chose to return. I was enjoying listening to the poets' renditions of their work. Suddenly an ethereal blonde woman walking on stage took my breath away. I couldn't believe what I was seeing. It was Guinie and she looked HAPPY! She looked stunning even; she glowed as she delivered the best performance of her life.

She scanned the room as she spoke, and her eyes stopped on me. I could see she recognized me! I beamed with pride as I smiled and waved to her. I ordered us our favorite tea, well at least I hoped it was still her favorite, I was sure it was.

She came and sat with me when she was done. She was grinning from ear to ear, I was right by the way; her cheeks dimpled deeply when she smiled fully. She sat down with a grace I'd not noticed the last time we'd taken tea together.

She took my hand and said, "I want to thank you. You helped me find my happy. It was never really lost, I merely lost sight of it for a little while, but it was always within me, just as you said. I searched my soul for the answers, and I looked to previous lessons to see what I had failed to learn. And I found my happy. I learned to quit looking to others and situations for my happiness. I learned to take pleasure in my own pursuits, to take pride in who I am and what I do and in myself. I am confident in who I am and the only person who has the power to take my happy away is me. So, knowing that, I shall not lose my happy again, I'm holding onto it for dear life. I am embracing it for all it's worth."

"I'm so glad Guinie! So happy for you" I gushed.

"I also know you; I've known you all along. I see you every morning when I face myself in the mirror. You are me. It took me a while to figure it out because I've ignored you for so long."

"Yes Guinie, I am your higher self. I am always with you; I never leave. I'm so glad that you heard me and took my advice. You found your happy because you listened to and believed in yourself!"

A CHRISTMAS TAIL

by Kathleen Long

The morning started out pretty normal, although this was the first Saturday I had free in 4 months and I planned on enjoying it as best as I could. I was 58 years old and just finished my second to last semester on the way to a degree. As I sat drinking my good morning cup of coffee and reading through the local paper, I started to notice all the holiday ads. It was only then that it hit me, Christmas was less than two weeks away, and because of my full-time work schedule and my weekend schoolwork, I hadn't shopped at all.

I flipped through the flyers and several of the items on sale would be perfect for gift-giving, and they were all on sale. I plotted out my day's journey and quickly showered. Getting dressed I simply dumped out the clothes from the basket and decided to fold them after I returned. Putting on my jacket, I grabbed my keys and with the list in hand, headed out to stop number one.

When I pulled into the parking lot I could tell everyone had the same idea as I did. I was hopeful they weren't after the same items. Stop one only had one item I wanted. That's why I decided to go there first. The parking lot was packed, but the weather outside was beautiful and actually a bit warmer than normal, so I didn't mind the extra walk.

Once inside I was surprised to find the store not nearly as crowded as I would have thought. I had to navigate the different isles and was able to locate the gift I was after. Each person I passed met me with a big grin and passing smile. What a great start to this adventure. I considered it a huge success, even though it was only one item off the list.

I quickly put my score into the car and I was off to store number two, which was where, with any luck, the majority of my list would be crossed off.

This time when I entered the parking lot the spaces were even more filled and as I circled around once or twice looking for a spot, I could see people coming and going non-stop at all the store entrances. My timing was perfect as I rounded the corner again and I was able to nab a spot only a few spaces up from the storefront.

Readying myself for battle I grabbed a cart along the way, double-checked my list, and went in.

What a difference from the last store. This time it was wall-to-wall shoppers.

I started up and down the aisles, again noticing everyone smiling and being so friendly. I remember thinking to myself, wouldn't it be wonderful if all year the atmosphere could be like this.

I found an entire center display with just books. I knew with my husband being an avid reader, I could find something for him for sure. Browsing the selections, I noticed a young mother pushing a cart with her young child in the seat. She seemed to keep turning to look at me and smiling. I wasn't sure what to feel but it did make me feel a bit uneasy. I wasn't sure why as people being friendly certainly wasn't a reason to make me feel that way.

As I went about my merry way, I noticed more and more stares coming in my direction. Many were accompanied by smiles and laughter. My thoughts went from everyone having Christmas cheer to me having an unexplained feeling of self-consciousness. But I knew my quest had to continue so off I went to find as many items as I could.

The smiles, smirks, and giggles continued the entire time as I made my way from aisle to aisle grabbing the items I had come there for. Despite my uneasy feeling, I had all the things I had written on my list in the cart.

Now the true adventure began. I made my way towards the front of the store and the registers. I swear half the town was in line waiting to get checked out. After a short game of eeny-meeny-miney-mo, I settled into a line. An elderly lady came in behind me and we got to talking about the upcoming holiday. That sure helped pass the time as it seemed the line moved pretty quickly and before I knew it I was up to the checkout. As I started placing my items on the belt and arranging them to have enough room, the woman I had been speaking with spoke up.

"You must have been in a hurry to get out of the house this morning."

I looked at her a bit confused and asked, "what do you mean?"

"You have a piece of clothing hanging down below your jacket and it looks like a tail."

Her reply seemed to echo off the walls and it felt as if the entire store had gone silent. As the words rendered, I turned to look behind me and sure enough, the old pair of pajama bottoms I changed out of this morning was sticking out from my coat. In my time getting dressed I must have pulled the bottoms into the waist of my jeans and because my coat was a bit longer, I didn't notice the extra feel on my backside.

Embarrassed was not a big enough word for how I felt. My cheeks were red and my face felt like I had spent all day in the Summer sun. It was as if I was moving in slow motion when I grabbed them, pulled them out, and stuffed them into my shoulder bag.

The cashier finished ringing up my things and I quickly helped bag them and placed them in my cart as I paid for them. I couldn't get out of there fast enough. As I turned to leave the sweet lady who let me know about my 'tail' waved to me and smiled.

"Merry Christmas, dear."

"You too, thank you."

With that, I was out. Of course, I had picked one of the registers furthest away from the exit doors and I just knew everyone I passed on my way out knew I was the lady with the pajamas sticking out of her ass. With my head down I just rushed out the best I could without any eye contact.

When I got to my car, I was still mortified but that feeling soon passed.

Looking back on that time, it was but one day of many. The situation gave me a great story to share with my grandchildren and provided so much comic relief over the years. Certainly, things could've been worse and they have been. You gain perspective over the years and having a pajama tail in the middle of a jammed packed department store isn't so bad when you think about it.

EXCELSIOR

by Kelli J Gavin

Jason Rodgers had loved the town of Excelsior, Minnesota for as long as he could remember. He grew up two blocks away from Lake Minnetonka and his first job was at the end of Water Street at the old Dock Theater. In high school, he loved walking home from the theater at night after the late show on the weekends. A few droplets of rain, the smell of leaves rustling in the fall, or even snowflakes falling on his nose. The dark nights of lake living were something he always treasured. The dark nights were also what inspired Jason to write stories until he couldn't keep his eyes open any longer, and sleep would overtake him. Those stories became larger than life once they were committed to paper.

Jason not only enjoyed helping customers at The Dock, but he also loved watching each of the movies that opened every two weeks. He always came up with a plan to make sure that he scheduled a time to view each of the films that would be showing in the small three-screen theater. Movies were what inspired him to write about his small town of Excelsior. Movies taught him the basics of good storytelling. Jason knew that he possessed the ability to create a compelling tale, but he also understood the importance of having a fine grasp of the English language.

Knowing that he wished to pursue writing, he enrolled in every English, Literature, and Creative Writing Class that he could find in the Minnetonka High School Class Catalogue.

Wanting to take advantage of as many classes as possible, he even enrolled in a few Community Education Classes in the evenings. Being the youngest student by far, the Community Education Instructor seemed to be enthralled with Jason's presence. Often asked to read his work out loud, he began experimenting with voices for each of his characters and diligently worked on character development and plot building. Once something he enjoyed doing, writing had become Jason's obsession. He woke in the morning and brainstormed about when he would find even a few moments in front of his laptop between school and work at the theater. He pulled out his laptop on the bus in the morning, during lunch in the vast lunchroom at Minnetonka High, and again on the bus ride home. He would quickly eat the dinner his mother prepared for him early each day before needing to leave for work. He joked with his mom and dad that his fingers itched when he had a good idea for a story and that they wouldn't stop itching until he had a chance to start writing it.

"Jason, I need help. You have to put your laptop away. I can't clean all three theaters myself. I am tired and want to go home. I still have homework to do tonight." Kerry Winger, his coworker explained begging for him to look up from the story he was writing.

"Kerry, I am sorry. I didn't even realize you were already working on the closing checklist. I love this story I am writing. Do you want to hear about it?" Jason asked excitedly hoping she would say she wanted to know all about it.

"Hard pass. Wait. No, I do want to hear about it. But I will make you a deal. I'll do theater pick up and sweeping if you clean the bathrooms. Then we can vacuum together to make sure we get it all done. When we finish, I will let you tell me all about your new, amazing, fantastic, best ever story you have written." Kerry smirked because she knew Jason would actually agree to her plan, bathrooms and all, just to be given the chance to tell her about and maybe even read a portion of his new work to her.

"Oh, my word. Yes. Deal. Also, you should know, there is gum in aisle three of theater two. Lots of gum. And the broom handle is on the fritz again. Grab some more duct tape and put it on the handle so I don't have to pick slivers out of your palms again." And with that, he was off to clean the bathrooms.

Kerry and Jason had enjoyed working together the past year at The Dock and had formed a true friendship. Neither seemed to be interested in the other for more than just friendship, and that made spending so much time together and working together that much easier. Kerry's mom was employed at Jason's dad's art supply store two blocks away from the Dock. She had worked for Mr. Rodgers since Kerry and Jason were in elementary school at Excelsior Elementary. Mrs. Winger needed help with Kerry when she was young, and Mrs. Rodgers volunteered to help watch her two days a week after school until Mrs. Winger's shift at the art supply store was complete. As a single mom, Mrs. Winger was thankful for the childcare help that was provided and for the job she adored. Being that Kerry and Jason had spent so much time together at school and then at Jason's house two afternoons a week, they joked that both were glad that they finally had a "sibling". Jason had always wanted a little brother, but he settled for the sister and friend that Kerry was.

As they finished the vacuuming, Jason offered to pull the two new slivers out of Kerry's hand. "I promise I will ask Ron tomorrow night to buy a new broom. I am sorry this one looks like it hurts so much. I am not sure I am going to be able to get the sliver out without making you bleed." Jason grimaced on Kerry's behalf.

"Just do what you can. Here are the tweezers. Distract me, tell me about your story." Kerry requested.

"So, this story is different. Everything I have ever written has been fiction. Made-up stories are meant to make the reader fall in love with a completely made up person or even a place. But this is mostly a true story. I feel we are lucky. Look where we live! Excelsior is such a beautiful old town, and right on Lake Minnetonka. We got to grow up here. We experience small town life every day. We know the people, the shop owners, the pastors at all the local churches. The teachers are friends with our parents. We know all the old tales of The Excelsior Amusement Park and when The Rolling Stones came to town. The history of our town remains alive and well known because of the dedicated residents that can't stop bragging about the home they love. I love this town and I think others will too. My book..." Jason was interrupted.

"Wait, I thought you said it was a story. Now it is a book? Ouch! Keep going." Kerry asked.

"It started as a story, and it grew. I've written about 75,000 words all about Excelsior. Some of the history and lore that has been passed down and then interrelated stories about people who live here in town. I wrote about Mr. Jimmy meeting Mick

Jagger at the soda counter. I wrote about the Reverend who doesn't seem to really like anybody but his mean cat named Molly. I even wrote about the Dock and working with you. I wrote about Excelsior, to honor the town and the people that I know and call friends, and some even family. I wrote about when your dad left and your mom started working at The Easel Art Supply Store. Each story has a reference to a person, a place, or even a season that can also be found in another story in the book. I feel like I am really on to something here." Jason's smile could light up a room when he spoke about the joy he found in writing.

Kerry couldn't help but smile back at him. "Jay, I wonder why the sudden change? All of sudden you are writing about true things, but you've never done that before. What inspired you?"

Jason paused, not really sure what to share. He knew he wanted to tell the truth, but didn't want to make it awkward. "You. You inspired me. You are my closest friend. I feel like I ignore you way too much. I am never fully engaged in our conversations, I sluff off and always let you do way more than your fair share here at work. You always tell me to keep writing. You encourage me to just keep working even when I don't believe in what I am writing. Thank you for showing me I can write well and for always being interested. Just thanks." Jason flushed quickly as his voice dropped off.

"Oh shut up. You are a good friend, and you know you can write. Stop being so sentimental and get the last sliver out."

He was right. He was lucky. Not just to live in the heartbreakingly beautiful town of Excelsior, but to have someone like Kerry who believed in him, and also told him to shut up when he started sounding too syrupy.

Continuing to write whenever he got a chance, those winter months seemed to fly by. Jason was discouraged when Kerry started receiving college acceptance letters, but one had yet to grace his mailbox. Kerry had her heart set on NYU but knew that she would have to apply for every grant and scholarship that was available and also work on campus to pay her tuition, for books and food. When an NYU decline arrived, Kerry was heartbroken. However, she knew that the U of M was still in her back pocket and she was prepared to make the best of it. Jason had continued working very hard and was always on the A Honor Roll. When a large envelope from Northwestern arrived, Jason was over the moon. His long-held dream of majoring in Journalism was actually being realized. Both Kerry and Jason finished out their senior year at the top of their class and graduated with honors from Minnetonka High. Mr. and Mrs. Rodgers and Mrs. Winger threw a joint graduation party as the Winger's had little family, but Kerry and Jason shared all the same friends. Northwestern and the U of M didn't know what was heading for them.

All throughout their undergraduate studies, Jason and Kerry remained as close as they had always been. Each taking the time to call and email throughout each week and support each other when things were challenging. Tough classes, lack of money, heartbreak when it came to relationships, the death of a grandparent. Kerry knew that Jason was only a phone call away. And Jason knew that Kerry was always his biggest fan, even from 8 hours north in the Twin Cities.

Kerry ended up completing her degree in just under three years. She had majored in Marketing and knew that graduate school was next in line. And of course, she also completed her

Doctorate in Business and Marketing Growth and Development in record time of just under two years. Jason finished his first four years and then an additional two and half years as completed his graduate studies in Journalism. While Jason chose to stay in Chicago after graduating, he still made at least one trip home to Excelsior about every 6 weeks and Kerry would travel down to see him whenever she was in between contracts. Their friendship remained strong and both thrived.

Jason never did complete his book about Excelsior. He struggled with wrapping it up and tying up the loose ends that he continued to stumble over. However, he kept it on his computer and promised himself that someday he would revisit it. That someday never happened. However, Jason loved having a syndicated column in numerous newspapers across the country, he wrote for many magazines and journals, and his current events blog with a bit of Midwest flavor became quite popular. Jason learned quickly that it was a luxury to live so comfortably and never have to search for work, as the work always found him. He experienced a bit of success with a trilogy book set he had published and enjoyed a devoted following of crazy fans.

"Excelsior" was never meant to be. Jason never did a great job of saving a second copy of his work, and rarely relied on cloud storage. When his apartment was broken into, of course, the first thing the thief took was his laptop, his flatscreen, and all the liquor from the cabinet. His work computer was always carried with him, so all of his professional writing was secure. Jason was really upset with himself for quite some time but knew that beating himself up over something he couldn't change would never benefit him. Jason made an asserted effort to increase his cloud storage and save everything twice from that day forward.

When Jason got the call from his mother that he needed to come home to Excelsior immediately, he dropped everything and was on the road within an hour. Mrs. Rodgers had explained over the phone that Jason's dad had suffered a mild heart attack, but then another and then a third within a 24 hour period. The stress on his heart of so many small events had knocked his heart out of rhythm and the external pacemaker wasn't able to do what it needed to do. There was still hope for healing, but his dad had a long road of recovery ahead of him. Knowing his mom couldn't handle the stress of taking care of her husband and driving him to doctor's visits and running the art supply store, Jason knew he needed to step in the gap and return home. But for how long? Jason knew that he would stay in Excelsior for as long as it took to help his dad be comfortable again and help his mom in any way he could.

By the time Jason reached the Fairview Southdale Hospital in Edina, the doctors explained that his father had suffered a fourth massive heart attack. A severe blockage was detected, but because of his fragile state, the doctors tried treating him with medications before performing the necessary surgery. They didn't feel he would have made it through surgery to unblock the two clogged arteries. When the fourth massive heart attack struck, there was no hope of reviving him and restarting his heart. Jason sat holding his mom around her shoulders and he trembled as she convulsed with tears. No hope. Jason just kept saying the words over and over again silently to himself. No hope.

A beautiful funeral was held and Mr. Rodgers was buried just outside of town. Mrs. Rodgers was mostly quiet following the days after her husband's passing. She kept thanking Jason for coming home and it made him quite uncomfortable. Did she not think that he would come home? His father had just died. Did she expect him to stay in Chicago? Quickly realizing he was edgy and defensive, he reminded himself to take a few deep breaths and to extend grace to mom in all she said and did in the coming days.

Mrs. Winger was so gracious and kind and kept the art supply store open for three weeks before Mrs. Rodgers felt ready to return. Mrs. Winger knew how to do the books, order inventory, and how to access the computer database for newsletter mailings and special sale email blasts. She had learned quickly and even made a few exceptional recommendations about annual planning and ideas about the upcoming year. Mrs. Rodgers was thrilled with her help. Mrs. Winger and Jason began running the store from 10 a.m. to 6 p.m Monday thru Saturday and with the help of Mrs. Rodgers and two teenagers after school and on Saturdays, a new normal rhythm was eventually achieved. Because the store carried many specialty items, relationships with return customers were their livelihood. Approximately four months after the funeral, Mrs. Rodgers was ready to resume teaching art classes in the evenings and on an occasional Saturday. The local artists were thrilled to see her again and adored having Jason back in town.

Jason was considering returning to Chicago as he had hired a full-time retired art teacher to take his place at the store. Really, the art teacher was hired to take his dad's place at the store. One evening as he was preparing a light dinner for his mom at home, his cell phone rang. He hated answering the phone but quickly went to see the name showing on the display. Kerry Winger. Jason swiftly answered the phone before the call went to voicemail.

After catching up a bit, Kerry's tone changed and she was then silent.

"Jason. I need to talk to you. Something has happened. I belong to a book club and I received the book list for 3 months about 5 months ago. I ordered the books off Amazon. Have you heard of the book "Newport" by Carl Clayson?" Kerry asked.

"Yep. I sure have. Didn't it just hit the New York Times best seller list? It has been on all the network morning shows and all over the internet." Jason answered.

"Jay, I read the book. I... I um... I don't really know how to tell you this, or how it has even happened... but, um..." Kerry continued to stammer.

"For the love, Kerry. Tell me!"

"Jay, "Newport" isn't really "Newport". I mean, the book that is supposed to be by Carl Clayson, is your book. It is "Excelsior."

"What are you talking about? There are similarities?" Jason asked.

"Jay, it isn't just a few similarities. It is almost everything. The name of the town has been changed, the lake isn't Lake Minnetonka, but a fictitious Swan Lake, and it isn't Mr. Jimmy meets Mick Jagger, but Miss Joni runs into the Grateful Dead. Some of the stories are so precise I would dare say that only the names have been changed. Jay, is it possible that Clayson stole your book? Maybe I've got it all wrong, but I don't understand. I read the book in a single sitting. Did you sell the rights to your book, and maybe not tell me? Jay, it is so good. It is one of the best books I have ever read. But this is your book. I...what happened?" Kerry's voice began to tremble.

Jason couldn't speak. He didn't have any answers to her questions. What was going on here? Was it possible that Carl Clayson, this best selling author, stole Jason's book? So many thoughts swimming in his head, he sat down before his legs gave way. The book was well written, but it wasn't "Excelsior." His "Excelsior". When did Kerry even get a chance to read and belong to a book club? Jason quickly stood with his phone held against his shoulder. Kerry continued to voice her disbelief and apologies but Jason didn't hear anything she was saying. Grabbing his laptop he quickly opened it and logged on to Amazon. He located "Newport", purchased it, and downloaded it immediately.

"I don't understand this. I can't even tell you what happened. I never showed my book to anyone other than you. Oh, no. No. Kerry, do you remember when I told you quite a few years back that my apartment had been broken into? My laptop containing "Excelsior" was on it. I made the stupid mistake of not saving it to a cloud or a zip drive. The book was on the laptop that was stolen. Kerry. I have to go. I will call you back." And with that, Jason hung up the phone.

Jason began reading immediately. He flushed red throughout his whole face and neck as he realized that this book, this copy called "Newport", was actually his book, almost verbatim. How? Why? How did Carl Clayson get his laptop? Who was Carl? Was he the man that stole the laptop all those years ago?

A simple google search produced listing after listing of "Newport", Best Seller, Carl Clayson, and his amazing first book. Deep pains began to rise in Jason's stomach. It was too late to call the publisher. It was too late to call his boss at the newspaper. He felt as if he was at a standstill. How would he ever prove that the book that had attained such fame was all a lie, and not Carl's, but his?

The next morning, Jason called Mrs. Winger at 8 a.m. He asked her if she would feel comfortable opening and closing the store. He thanked her and explained that he had some work to do and it couldn't wait. Mrs. Winger was happy to oblige.

Jason spent the day on the phone and using the internet. He read the entire book that he downloaded again, copied it, circled everything in red that had been changed, and ran to the print shop down the street to ask them to print out the entire book. He called his friend and attorney in Chicago and explained what was brought to his attention, repeated the story three times, and voiced his concerns about not knowing how Clayson got his hands on "Excelsior" in the first place. Jason was advised to not contact the publisher directly, nor Clayson. His attorney would take care of it. Jason wrote out all of the parallels and felt he had a solid case to help prove that "Excelsior" was his. He forwarded a copy of the book, with all the highlighted information to his attorney and rubbed his eyes.

While reminding himself to stay calm, he knew he needed to call Kerry. He needed to tell her what was happening and to thank her for calling him in the first place. If Kerry had never stumbled upon this book from the book club she joined, Jason very well would have remained clueless. He had been consumed with work and writing for so long, that most of what he read in those days was on the internet.

Clearing his throat, he took a few deep breaths. "Jay, is that you? I was worried when I didn't hear back from you. Are you okay? What is going on?" Kerry blurted before Jason had a chance to say hello.

Jason filled her in on everything he had done, about the attorney and that he was advised not to contact the publisher or Clayson directly. He shared that a deposition would be required and was advised to keep notes about everything that occurred concerning the book.

"Jason, I'm sorry. Know this. I knew way back when we were in high school that you were an amazing writer. I know I joked and made fun of you because writing was all you ever spoke of. But this book, your book, it is breathtaking. Even with Newport thrown in here and there, I could see myself walking the downtown streets and down to the lake. You captured our hometown like only you could. I will support you in any way that I can." Kerry shed a few tears.

The next morning, Mrs. Winger made a beeline for Jason as she entered the store.

"I am so sorry. I talked to Kerry last night and she filled me in. You will not believe this, but Carl Clayson is expected to be at the Excelsior Bookstore next Friday night. He is doing a speaking promotional tour in small Minnesota towns as he continues to promote his book. I mean "Newport". We should attend, don't you think?" Mrs. Winger smirked.

Jason couldn't believe that Clayson would still honor the commitment in Excelsior once he became aware of the accusations of theft and plagiarism. But Jason couldn't stay away if he tried. He looked forward to seeing this phony face to face.

Kerry unexpectedly arrived at the shop at 6:30 p.m.. Informing her mother and Jason that there wasn't any place she would rather be, she linked arms with them as they walked down Water Street to the bookstore.

"Do you think his publisher has informed him that you have been in contact with them?" Kerry inquired.

"I don't think he would know as of yet. Why would he think he could show up in Excelsior?"

The door chimed as they entered the bookstore. Many local Excelsior residents were milling about and chatting in small groups. Wine and appetizers were served and the bookstore owner Midge quickly approached Jason.

"Hello and welcome! We are so happy you are here, Jason. Our own small town writer! Mrs. Winger and Kerry, so nice to see you also. Please come in, enjoy some treats, and have a great evening." Midge excused herself as she prepared to get the evening underway.

When Carl Clayson took the podium, he was met with a round of applause. Everyone seemed to be excited to see him and was clapping. Even Kerry's slow, loud, sarcastic clap added to the momentum of the evening.

"Thank you for having me here tonight. What an honor. I thought I would start by reading a few selected portions of "Newport" and then we will have plenty of time for questions." Clayson began.

Jason grimaced as Clayson read his own words. Some paragraphs were word for word. Each portion that was read was met by additional applause. When the Q & A portion of the evening began, Clayson easily fell into a comfortable conversation with the crowd. He was endearing and allowed time for each person to feel special.

When a slight pause in the conversation occurred, Jason stood. "Mr. Clayson, Jason Rodgers. The story about Miss Joni meeting the Grateful Dead. I found it to be so similar to our own Mr. Jimmy meeting Mick Jagger. What year did the Grateful Dead travel through Newport?"

Carl cleared his throat and took a drink of water. "Well, ahem, isn't that a great tidbit? I love small town stories that seem to be passed on. Not sure about the year, but I will ask Miss Joni next time I see her." A few people giggled.

"Mr. Clayson, one last question. When did you decide to change the Reverend's cat's name to Missy instead of Molly? You shouldn't have changed that name. Molly has such a ring to it." Jason never broke eye contact even with Kerry pulling at his elbow trying to make him sit down.

"This evening has been nothing short of amazing. Thank you for having me! Excuse me as I take a short break and then will return for signings." Clayson quickly excused himself for the restroom located just past the storeroom.

Bridgit Patterson, Clayson's manager and agent, stormed towards Jason. "I am not sure why you are being so confrontational, but I will need to ask you to leave."

Kerry glared at Bridgit, "But Mr. Clayson promised to meet with every person and sign every book."

"All three of you should leave now before I call the police and report you for disturbing the peace." Bridgit sneered.

Mrs. Winger had made her way to the door before Kerry finally convinced Jason that they needed to leave.

As they again walked arm in arm slowly down Water street, they heard someone shout, "Mr. Rodgers! Please wait!"

Jason turned to see Carl Clayson jogging down Water Street towards them.

As he caught his breath, Carl's words came slowly, "I can tell it was you that wrote this book. Who defends a book more than the writer himself? Listen. I was paid to say I wrote this. We changed the name of the town, the names of people and a few facts here and there. I was told that my paycheck would increase every year if the book did well and as long as I could keep up publicity tours on behalf of the publishing company."

"The publishing company paid you to lie? To steal, to rob me and break into my home?"

"Rob you? What are you talking about? I never stole from your home or broke in. The publisher approached my agent, and my agent persuaded me. I have no clue how they came into possession of the book." Clayson declared.

Jason believed him. Clayson was a liar and a persuasive, well-paid frontman. "I won't be discussing this any further with you. As we speak, my attorneys are already in contact with your publisher. "Excelsior" was the first book I ever wrote. I struggled, I toiled, I put it away and ignored it. But I was never given the chance to finish it. You took that from me. You may not have been the one to break into my apartment, but you stole from me. My book, my life, even the town Excelsior. Good luck to you. You are going to need it."

Jason, Kerry, and Mrs. Winger continued walking down Waterstreet. Away from Mr. Clayson. Away from "Newport".

An undisclosed settlement had been reached and Jason knew that by signing the documents, he would never be able to stake his claim on the first book he had ever written or speak publicly about the town of Newport actually being the town of Excelsior. By signing, not only was he awarded a large settlement, he was also given peace. Peace of mind that he did the right thing. He never wanted to be famous, he only wanted to write well. And the fact that "Newport" continued to sell and remained on the NYT's bestseller list for 19 months confirmed what he already knew. "Excelsior" was the best piece he had even written to date.

Opening his laptop, Jason began writing. Fast and furious the words flowed out of him. Feeling hopeful again, he knew there just might be another book or two in him.

EVER AFTER

by Lyssa Damon

They say rain on your wedding day is meant to be a sign of good luck. It leaked into my shoes and ruined my hair. The hairstylist had struggled to tame my wayward curls, but even the endless packs of bobby pins and clouds of hairspray couldn't save it in the end. Kiss-proof lipstick in 'Cherries in the Snow' and waterproof mascara. Or so the bottle proclaimed.

An outside wedding and we somehow chose the first rainy day of the season. Perhaps stilettos had not been the wisest shoe choice for walking on grass, but who chooses wedding shoes for their practicality? I walked up the petal scattered aisle as it started to drizzle.

"Do you, Cameron Hunter Gilana take Juliet Camille Carter to be your lawfully wedded wife?" He did.

No sooner had we said our 'I dos' than it started to pour.

"I now pronounce you Mr. and Mrs. Gilana."

Everyone ran for cover before the minister had a chance to say, "You may now kiss the bride."

Did he say it later? I forget.

Champagne flowed. No one noticed that my mascara was smudged or that my husband danced most of the night with every woman but me.

They say love overcomes all. Today is our fifth wedding anniversary. We've been through so much and here we are. In this new home. The white Italian tiles are elegant, but more your style than mine. The whole house is just as you described it to me on our honeymoon, including the winding staircase with the steel banister. All of it. There is a fancy plaque at the front door. 'C & J'. I trace the engraved letters, running my fingers over each one. I smile.

The caterers busy themselves setting up the fancy snacks and drinks. Crystal champagne flutes, tiny silver cocktail forks, and linen serviettes. Impressive. They make all of this look easy. Bunches of fresh red roses. Red is pretty, but pink roses have always been my favourite.

Prints of our wedding photos. So elegant. So cleverly edited to hide the chaos of that day. Smiles and joy are the memories that were captured. The perfect final touch to decorate the tables.

No one seems to mind that I am singing out loud and a little out of tune. Our song. My Immortal.

Caspian is under the main table, hoping for a treat. He sees me and leaves his hiding place to weave between my ankles. Silly boy. He's purring like an engine. One of the catering staff sees him and shoos him out of the room. I don't protest. There is much to do and Caspian, no doubt, has his eye on the sushi platter.

The guests will be arriving soon. I want everything to be perfect. I smile into the mirror and admire the diamond earrings you gave me for our first anniversary. You always loved my curls. You complained when I started straightening my hair. I preferred my curls tamed. Tonight my auburn curls are just for you.

I hear voices downstairs. Snippets of conversation and much admiration for the new house. I'm not quite ready to join the festivities. This is the perfect spot, in the shadows by the balustrade. I can see without being seen.

There you are. So handsome in your tux. Keeping the crowd entertained. I see some familiar faces. I see HER. She's beautiful. Perfectly put together. Her smooth, platinum hair cascades over her tanned shoulders. Your hand in the small of her back. You think I don't notice.

I remember the day I headed into the storm to look for you. The day before our third anniversary. The rhythmic sound of the windshield wipers, tears hot on my cheeks.

The weather much like our wedding day. We had had another fight. So many fights. You were distant and insisted on going for a drive to clear your head. You had been gone for hours. I found your car parked at the beach, overlooking the ocean. Relief was replaced with confusion, then rage as I realized you were not alone, that SHE was in the car with you, your bodies entwined. I don't know if either of you noticed me speeding away. The delivery truck didn't notice me, and I couldn't see through the tears.

I don't remember much. Twisted metal. Flashing lights. Red and blue. Blinding me. I don't want to remember. Tonight is a celebration of this beautiful new home, of us.

Something catches your attention. You've spotted the photos. You rifle through them. A nice surprise, my love?

You start up the stairs at about the same time I begin my descent, our wedding pictures in your hand. You don't notice me.

As you reach the landing, I reach for your hand and guide it around my waist. Your blue eyes are wide, you say my name as I pull you close and kiss you hard on the mouth. I breathe you in. The landing is wide enough for us to dance. We dance. I lead.

A scream shatters the party vibe. It's her. She is hunched over a figure at the foot of the stairs. A crumpled, broken body.

You are here, with me. Caspian weaves between your ankles, purring. We watch the guests gather around. Someone calls 911 about an accident. She sobs. A woman I don't recognize comforts her.

"Shhhhh Jessica. Breathe." She is inconsolable.

We watch paramedics arrive and try to revive the fallen man. They pronounce him dead.

The police arrive.

"Sorry ma'am", the older of the two uniformed men addresses her.

"I know you're upset, but we need to ask you a few questions. Did you see anyone on the stairs with Mr. Gilana? "

"There was no one there. He called out Juliet's name."

"Who is Juliet?"

"She was his wife."

"Come, my love, it's time to go."

I take your hand. Kiss your cheek and watch the penny drop. You recognize him now.

"Was?"

"She died in a car accident two years ago."

ETERNAL FLAME

by Lyssa Damon

Jonathan Keet shuffled off this mortal coil on a Wednesday afternoon, three days shy of his eighty-ninth birthday.

Logan found himself on a road trip to the old boy's funeral. How fitting that he should be making this trip in Selena, the 1962 Mercedes-Benz 190-SL gifted to him by his grandfather last Christmas.

"I know you'll treasure her as I always have."

Grandad had named his car after the love of his life. Selena, the grandmother Logan never got to meet, although he knew her through the many stories Grandpa told. Logan smiled, thinking that grandpa was finally with his beloved again.

'My Selena's eyes were as blue as the car, that's how they came to share a name.' My two goddesses.

Gran and Grandpa married in 1962. They bought the car that same year. Years passed. A son. Two daughters, eight grandchildren, one grandson - born last, three months after Selena died.

The road was long, but there was little traffic and Selena was filled with memories. She smelled of leather, cherry and maple pipe tobacco. Logan didn't smoke but he kept a pouch of Grandpa's tobacco in the glove compartment. He breathed deeply and replayed the many hours spent with grandpa, chatting, polishing the vintage beauty, and drinking cola out of glass bottles.

So many years ago. Before life happened and Logan only saw Grandpa at family gatherings. Even more seldom since Logan and Gail's divorce. Grandpa believed in the magic of true love. Logan no longer did.

'Callie Inn'

He followed the signs and pulled up outside just as dusk turned to darkness. Selena looked every bit the elegant grande dame, parked outside the quaint stone building.

The interior of the inn, just as beautiful as the outside. A curry dinner - Grandpa's favourite. An after dinner whiskey.

"Cheers Grandpa. I hope you find your Selena."

A good night's rest.

He dreamed of Grandpa.

Breakfast was delicious. Logan noticed a couple at the next table, obviously in love. He overheard snippets of conversation.

'Honeymoon..'

'Forever..'

As he got up, the young man called to him.

"Excuse me Sir, is that your car out front?"

The couple asked for a few photos of them in the car, a honeymoon keepsake after a long separation. Logan obliged; a few happy snaps. Some on his phone, some on a beautiful vintage camera the young man had. The young couple's love was evident. It almost made him forget that love didn't exist.

Soon enough, Logan was on his way.

It was a rare occasion that the family came together. That evening, Logan and his mom leafed through piles of photos that Mom had found stashed away. Photos his mother had not seen in decades.

"I just assumed they'd been lost in the fire."

The house fire shortly after Selena's death had stolen many memories.

A faded photo caught his eye. His car parked in front of...could it be? The sign confirmed it. Callie Inn. He flipped the photo over. 'Honeymoon". The next photo made him catch his breath. Grandpa and Grandma. Fresh-faced, smiling. Familiar.

He pulled out his phone.

"Aaaah grandpa, you found her."

LOST & FOUND

by Sam Palmer

"Oh look at those flowers!" Madeleine rushed over to the trough filled with flowers, leaning down and smelling the blooms. "They smell divine! George, come smell these!"

Hands still in my pocket I leaned down and inhaled through my nose "Mmmmm, very nice."

"We should plant some at our house!" she looked at me beaming.

"You don't garden."

"Well," she turned away, placing her hands on her hips looking down at the trough. "I suppose I'll have to learn then!"

"Alright," I laughed, looking down at my watch. "Come on, the flyer said the estate sale is from noon to three."

Madeleine grabbed my hand, shooting one final look over her shoulder at the flowers as we made our way up the dirt path to the old white house. The paint was chipping, and it looked like it needed a new roof. A few yards away was the barn, once red it now stood brown and weathered, parts of the grooved wood still clinging to the last strips of paint.

"Oh George, I just love it out here in the country!" she sighed, looking at the surrounding land covered in tall grass, caged in by wooden posts and barbed wire.

"It's very nice," I threw an arm around her shoulders and she leaned into me as we climbed the stairs of the front porch, the planks creaking beneath our feet.

"Oh! Look!" she squealed, pulling away from me and rushing inside the open door where a few others were already perusing the items for sale. I shook my head, removing my hat as I crossed the threshold and into the dark house.

The light came pushing through the dingy lace curtains that still hung on the windows. The place smelled like someone had recently cleaned but not quite managed to mask the smell of mothballs and gun oil. Madeleine stood in front of a table that held various odds and ends for sale.

"Maddy, this is all junk," I leaned in.

"How can you say that, George? These are treasures! Look at this," she gingerly picked up a white china teapot, covered in hairline cracks and fading blue flowers. I watched as Madeleine turned it over in her hands soaking up the details as if it were the most marvelous thing she had ever seen.

The price tag, a white card tied to the handle of the teapot, fell forward through her hands. Reaching out, I held it between my fingers, tilting it towards me.

"10 dollars?!" I whispered. "These people are out of their minds!"

"Oh George," she scolded. "Don't be such a miser."

I felt a slight relief as she set it back down and continued looking through the trinkets on the table. I looked down and began to inspect the 'treasures' more closely. A whole box of old thimbles, another full of buttons varying in colors and sizes. I smirked as I picked up an old wooden yoyo, scuffed and paint faded. Shaking my head, I set it back down and moved further down the table. That's when it happened.

My breath caught in my throat, hand shaking as I reached out slowly, grabbing the scruffy neck of the blue stuffed bunny. The fur felt old and rough but familiar in my hands. I stared down at its dirty face, one of his black beaded eyes torn off and missing, leaving just the strings that had once held it protruding and meaningless. His once pink nose now dingy and stained. One of the ears had been ripped and I ran a thumb over the red thread that had been used to repair it. For a moment, I was transported to a distant memory. Sitting at my mother's feet as she opened her sewing box, pulling out the spool of cherry red thread.

"George?"

The noise of the people walking and talking around us in the foyer of the old white house came rushing in. I blinked rapidly, trying to swallow as I turned to see Madeleine's brown eyes filled with concern.

"Are you alright?" she whispered.

"Madeleine," I choked. "The bunny. This was Paul's."

My lip trembled as her eyes moved down at the old stuffed animal in my grip.

"I don't know how it's possible, but I'm telling you this is Paul's rabbit, Stanley. He took this thing everywhere."

"But I thought Paul had it with him when-"

"He did. The night he went missing, he had it with him. I'm sure of it, Maddy. We checked everywhere for this damn rabbit, and it was never found."

I straightened up and looked around the room, blinking back more tears as the memories and horror of that time of my childhood came flooding in. Madeleine touched the tip of the rabbit's ear, rubbing it between her fingers before turning to me and placing a hand on my chest.

“It must be a stuffed rabbit just like Stanley. I mean, it's not like they only made one of these little guys, right?" she offered a smile, but I shook my head looking down.

"This IS Stanley, Maddy. That red stitching there on his ear, that's where my mother sewed the tear from when I'd tried to take Stanley out of Paul's hands."

"Darling, that was so long ago-"

"No, I know it, Maddy. I know it! This is Stanley!" my voice began to rise as I gripped the rabbit tighter.

Madeleine rubbed my shoulder as she looked around the room, smiling and nodding to a couple that was passing us. I turned the rabbit over in my hands, his ears flopping forward as I searched for the tag I knew would be sewn into the seam of his left leg. Pinching it between my fingers, I felt the blood leave my face. I looked up at Madeleine, tears no longer contained as I held up the tag for her to read. Faded and barely still legible written in crude children's handwriting with a black marker spelled: PAUL.

WITNESS

by Sam Palmer

I loved the night. It meant the house was mine and mine alone. To do what I pleased; running, jumping, knocking things over. This house became my personal playground without the risk of being told "no", kids trying to pick me up, the sound of screams and squeals, or any other obnoxious noises the small ones tended to make. I could definitely live without the Little ones, not that I had much of a choice. I suppose they were here before me. At least, the older of the two Littles was. "Michael" they called him. I didn't much care for that one. He smelled like sour milk to me. He was always grabbing and pulling and poking. The smaller little, "Emma" wasn't so bad. She didn't do much. Just ate, and slept really. That was my kind of Little.

I sat in the dark on the windowsill, looking down at the sidewalk below. Nothing going on out there. I wonder if the Bigs remembered to fill my food bowl before they went to bed. I jumped down and ran into the food room. Launching myself onto the carpet, I could feel it slide across the tile beneath my feet. I came to a stop and stepped off the rug, leaving it in a crumpled pile behind me. My bowl was full! I lowered my body, bringing my face closer to the dish, and let my tail dance back and forth behind me. I began munching on my food happily. I loved the Bigs. Sometimes.

A little later, I sat on the counter cleaning myself. I knew full well I wasn't supposed to, but at night, there were no laws. If I wanted to sit here licking my paws and cleaning my face, then that's just what I was going to do. One of the Bigs would usually accuse me of being "filthy" and that my presence on the counter was "disgusting", followed by a "shoo!". I'd seen some of the things they do with their front paws, and how they could accuse ME of being the filthy one, I never understood.

My ears twitched and brought my grooming to a halt as I heard the low rumble of movement upstairs. thump thump thump There it was again. My eyes darted to the window to see if the sun was starting to come up. No, it was still in the dead of night. Far too late for the Bigs or the Littles to be up. Better go investigate. I hopped down off the counter and walked across the tile until I reached the stairs. I placed my front paw on the first step and waited, listening intently. My ears pivoted around, tuning in to hear even the slightest movement. Nothing. I darted up the stairs, my padded feet absorbing any noise. I knew exactly where the floor creaked at the top of the stairs, so I carefully maneuvered around it and stopped in the dark hallway. I paused, waiting again for a noise.

SQUEAK

My left ear turned facing the noise and my eyes followed. It came from Emma's room. I walked down the hall and saw the door just cracked. I slowly stepped forward to peer inside. The light plugged into the socket on the far wall illuminated the tiny room with a soft glow. Casting shadows in every direction. Stuffed animals, rocking chair, dresser, changing table, crib....the crib. Something wasn't right about the crib. I stepped in slowly to get a better look. Standing over the crib was Michael. He was standing on his tiptoes, hands clasping the railing and looking down at Emma. Just inside the door, I sat down staring at him, tail twitching in curiosity behind me. He hadn't noticed me enter the room, and I could hear him talking.

"I know I'm supposed to love you. But I don't. I waited and waited but I still don't. I hate you. Before you, Dad used to play with me, and Mom would always tuck me in and snug me before bed. Then you had to go and show up. We don't need you. Everything was better before. I hate you."

Michael got quiet still standing over the crib. I thought maybe he'd fallen asleep. I'd seen him do it once, when he was smaller, right into a bowl of food. Face first, like some kind of beast. He hadn't done that in a while, but he was still a beast. I, truthfully, wasn't surprised to hear him say such awful things to Emma. That's just the kind of Little he was. Sour milk, I'm telling you. I'd seen him pinch her when the Bigs weren't looking, or push her over. He was always doing awful things. He once tried to cut my tail off with a pair of scissors. I wish the Big had eaten that one at birth. Some things just get born rotten. And Michael was rotten.

He apparently had not fallen asleep because I saw his arm reach down into the crib. I kept watching as he slowly grabbed hold of something. He stood up even taller on his tiptoes to lean further into the crib, this time with both hands. It looked like he was holding something down. What was this terrible thing up to? I walked across the room and jumped up onto the tall dresser. I was still behind him, to his left now, and up higher with a clear view into the crib. Michael was holding a stuffed elephant flush against Emma's face. An odd thing to do, she's too small to move it, how would she breathe? I could hear him grunt as he tried to balance on his toes, still holding the elephant down.

I walked to the edge of the dresser and leaned forward, feeling anxious about how long he'd been holding the stuffed animal against her face. I could feel the danger in the air, and I became very concerned for Emma. He would kill her if he didn't move it. Finally, not being able to take it anymore, I let out a loud 'Meow!'. Michael jumped, releasing the elephant and stumbling back onto the flats of his feet. We looked at each other for a brief moment, then he turned and ran out of the room. thump thump thump until I heard him push his door open squeak and jump into his bed thud.

I jumped down off the dresser, crossing the room until I was at the base of the crib. Peering back at the door, I checked to be sure he wasn't there, then looked up at the rail and jumped, perfectly clearing the top of the crib and landing gently onto the soft mattress inside. Emma was lying on her back, arms up by her head, face turned facing the wall. There was a blanket by her feet, and the stuffed elephant lay by her neck, one stuffed leg laying across her shoulder. Standing completely still, eyes wide, ears alert; I waited, listening for any noises. Nothing. I watched her, expecting to see her move or a quiet snore to escape from her, but nothing.

I stepped forward and smelled her foot–smelled like Emma. She always smelled like soap and food. But there was something else too. What was that scent? I sniffed some more, still not recognizing that smell. I moved farther up the bed, slowly, until I got to her head. I looked down at her. She looked like she was sleeping, but.... something wasn't right. I leaned forward and smelled her upper lip. There was no soft breath coming from her nose tickling my whiskers. I looked at her chest. There was no slow rising and falling of her sleepy, rhythmic breathing. I'd never smelled it before which is why I hadn't recognized it, but I knew now that the underlying smell was Death.

I quickly retreated from the lifeless lump in the crib and hopped over the rail and back to the floor. I darted out of the room and into the dark hallway. I had to let the Bigs know. "Meow! Meow! Meow!" I turned in circles, letting out my loud call. I could hear it echoing and bouncing off the walls of the hallway and filling the quiet house. "MEOW! MEOW!" The rustling of the sheets coming from the Bigs room. The light under the doorway flicking on.

"That god damn cat..." a groggy voice said from behind the door.

"MEOW! MEOW! MEOW!"

"Well, what does he want?"

"How the Hell would I know?"

"MEOW!"

"Jesus Christ! Okay, Spencer, I'm coming!"

"We should've gotten a dog..."

THUMP THUMP THUMP

The slow heavy footsteps got closer to the door until finally it opened and a disheveled Big stood in front of me. I looked up at her, turning in circles and continuing my obnoxious song. I wanted her to follow me. She had to see what that rotten Little did to Emma.

"Meow!! Meow!"

She took a step forward, rubbing her eyes "Spencer! Stop it! I swear if you wake the baby, I'm putting you outside..," she hissed at me. I continued walking down the hall, and she started towards me. I stopped in front of Emma's room until she was just about to reach me.

"Spencer," she whispered "Please don't go in there. No! Come on-"

I ignored her, and pushed the door open, running into the room and stopping at the crib. I looked back to be sure she was following me. The Big stood in the doorway, eyes alert now, and pleading with me to be quiet. "Spencer! Come here, baby! Don't jump into that-"

I hopped up and swiftly landed into the crib. I could hear as she came bounding across the room, reaching in and grabbing me. It was clumsy and quick, my legs going everywhere. I hissed and instinctively bit her until she whispered "Ow!" and released me. I hit the ground with a thud and ran to the door and stopped. I turned and watched as the Big looked at her hand, checking for blood from my bite. Not finding any, she rested her hands on the rail of the crib and leaned down. She appeared to be relieved, thinking Emma hadn't been woken. I saw her body relax, and she leaned forward grabbing the edge of the blanket and pulling it higher to Emma's chest.

Suddenly, I saw her body tense up and I could hear her heart skip a beat. She rested her hand on Emma's tiny chest and immediately knew something was wrong. I saw her body move as she began to gently shake Emma, trying to wake her.

"Emma?" I could smell the sweat, and fear as her voice got louder.

"Emma? Emma, wake up!" She reached both hands into the crib and picked up Emma. I sat in the doorway, ears flat, and hair raised as the Little's head rolled back and arms and legs dangled limp in the now screaming Big's hands. "EMMA?! OH MY GOD! EMMA!" her trembling voice pierced the night, and I heard the loud footsteps of the other Big come running into the room.

"Dawn? What the Hell-" he paused as he entered the room, absorbing the scene. I saw as reality swept over his face and then fear. In one movement, he was across the room, now cradling Emma in his own arms trying to nudge her awake.

"Emma, sweetie, come on. Wake up, baby. Wake up for, Daddy," he had her pressed against his chest and patting her back. I'd seen him do this many times, usually after she had eaten. The Bigs were both crying now, and one ran out of the room and grabbed a phone. She was yelling into it "MY BABY ISN'T BREATHING! PLEASE! HURRY!"

The rest of the night was filled with more crying and screaming. Strangers showed up and filled Emma's room. I was kicked out and left in the hallway. I don't know what happened in there, but the Big let out a loud scream that sent shivers through my body and I ran and hid under the Big's bed. I heard a lot more footsteps, some quiet talking, and muffled cries. Then I heard a squeak as a door opened. Michael.

I came out from under the bed and crept to the doorway. I saw as he poked his head out of his room. There were still people coming and going and he was watching with curious eyes. His eyes landed on me down the hall and we stared at each other for several moments. His eyes narrowed, and I could feel him boiling under the surface with hatred and rottenness. They had to know it was him! "MEOW!" I let out my loud call, and Michael's eyes got big as if he knew I was trying to tell on him. "MEOW! MEOW!"

"That god damn cat again!" and a Big came out of Emma's room with fists clenched. He noticed Michael first though, and immediately the anger washed from his face and was replaced with grief like I had never seen. He dropped to his knees, pulling Michael into him, and began sobbing. I could still see Michael's face over the Big's shoulders and we met eyes again.

"Michael, buddy, Michael….it's….it's all going to be okay. Okay, buddy? We love you so much. I'm so sorry-" the Big was spitting out words between sobs, his whole body shaking as he squeezed onto the Little. Michael stared back at me blankly, mouth agape, caught completely off guard by the Big's raw emotions. Like a flash of lightning, I saw as the thought hit him and he realized he'd gotten away with killing Emma. His eyes crinkled as his face broke into a smile, and he threw his arms around the Big, who was now uncontrollably crying.

Just then the other Big and a man dressed in all black came walking out of Emma's room. She looked down and saw Michael and fell right alongside the other Big on her knees, throwing her arms around both of them and burying her head into his neck. The two Big's cries and muffled apologies to Michael as they tried to explain to him that his little sister had died in her sleep, was enough to break any heart. Michael never said a word through his parent's tearful explanation. Not until he finally interrupted them, leaning back and asking "What's SIDS?"

JUST PRESS PLAY

by Jay Long

I am Airmen First Class, William C. Mitchel. For the last 37 weeks, I have been stationed in a remote area off the coast that our command has deemed Renaissance island. Our initial mission was to reconnect the area to an off-shore power grid that was damaged during a rather harsh winter.

Nothing prepared us for what transpired while we were here.

The hum of the transport engine was all I could hear. Which was both good and bad. It helped drown out the sound of my heart beating a million miles an hour in my ears but I had all I could do to hear Staff Sergeant Kendall going over the mission specs one last time.

Two days ago, an allied airbase used as the center of operations was attacked when several missiles destroyed the airport and much of the surrounding downtown area stood in ruin from the blasts. Luckily the hospital was untouched but there was no way out of the city. Militia leaders had started to move troops in from the hills and surrounding farmlands through an underground tunnel system and utilizing bunkers as strongholds throughout the region.

To this point, the reason why we had units in Wittenburg was classified and only known to those deployed to the city. A cache of plutonium was being moved there and stored. Somehow the militia leaders became aware of this and began taking bids from other countries of power.

It was now our duty to supply additional troops with boots on the ground to help stave off the advance, extract our units, and safely escort the shipment once the area was again stable.

As the jump door opened, everything seemed to go silent and movements were in slow motion. It was as if I was standing outside of my body watching the scene inside the carrier unfold before my eyes. The only problem was, I wasn't watching. This was it, I was there, standing, waiting for my OK to go.

The atmosphere surrounding the drop zone made it nearly impossible for our transport to fly below 15,000 feet making this my first HALO jump; high altitude, low opening, since the academy. In ten seconds I would be at the mercy of the wind and dependent on my training for the 4 minutes it would take to reach the ground.

The jumpmaster gave me the thumbs up and I found myself suspended in the air. I remember thinking, this must be what it feels like to experience zero gravity. That thought soon passed as I found myself in an accelerated free fall, trying to gain my senses of where I was and to find my center.

Below me was the drop zone covered in tinted green smoke rising up to where I was. I entered the cloud cover for a brief moment before seeing what awaited me below. Fires off in the distance. The sounds of gunfire echoed. The landing zone was becoming clearer, although those on the ground still resembled something you see in a simulated video game.

I deployed my shoot and began gliding focusing on a safe spot for me to land. It was then I noticed flashes coming from the ground towards the group of soldiers I had jumped with. There were snipers trying to take us out before we even landed. The seriousness of the situation took a huge turn. I saw several of my fellow paratroopers go limp mid-descent. I was now steering myself in mid-air turns hoping to drop quicker and get myself to the safety of some type of cover as soon as possible. The snipers were hitting more and more of us out of the sky. I decided then to cut my main shoot to become less visible. I stayed in free fall for as long as I could and just as I reached 700 feet, I deployed my reserve shoot which I used to get myself safely on the ground.

I was alone gathering my gear when a lifeless body hit the ground next to me. It rattled me but lit a fire under my ass and I jumped behind the first wall I could find. I observed my area and then beat feet the thirty yards to my west where transport vehicles awaited us.

A make-shift command center had been set up just next to the hospital. We were lead into one of the two large white tents that served as both a rallying point for those heading into the fight and emergency triage for those returning injured.

I heard my name called out by the Group Commander

"Mitchel!"

"Sir!"

"Report to the hospital roof and eliminate any threats to our north"

"Yes, Sir!"

I had 8 flights of stairs to think about the rest of my life. I was going through the inventory in my head and the steps I needed to take once I reached my perch. The stairwell insulted me from the goings-on outside. The thick concrete walls muffled the bomb blasts and gunfire but with each floor I reached, the sounds seemed to get more clear. My life was about to change once again. I finally reached the deck, my lungs filled with the burnt air that hovered over the entire area. I reported to the CO and readied my gear.

"Billy, dinner's ready."
"OK Mom, I'll be right there."

Pressing pause on the game, I set the controller on the charger and headed down the hallway. Saving the world would have to wait a few more minutes.

THE HOUSE

by Nicole Labonte

The house lay abandoned, untouched for many years, except for the rodents who had found solace in the silence there. Secrets of the home well hidden within the walls, but about to be discovered.

Jacob and Mason stumbled upon the house one hot day in July, almost missed for the trees hung low over the roof, and the grass stood tall, easy to miss from the road passing by. The two of them had been exploring abandoned houses for many years.

The house was the size of a trailer, long but very narrow, with grey siding and a black roof. The two friends made their way through the soaring grass, stumbling through random holes in the ground, but eventually made it safely. The steps that led up to the front door had long crumbled into the earth below, but they managed to get to it unscathed and opened both doors leading inside. Once inside, they both felt and an overwhelming sense of dread enveloped them, almost as if the house was telling them they shouldn't be there, but they brushed the feelings aside without mentioning it to the other and continued on with their adventure.

Inside the smell was horrendous; mold covered the walls, dust scattered throughout the first room; the living room. A small rug lay on top of an unfinished wooden floor which was covered in rodent droppings, not much had been left behind in this room except for the rug and a ripped-up old couch. As they walked through the living room, they were cautious not to disturb anything or fall through the old and unsteady flooring.

"Jacob, it smells nasty in here," Mason commented as he pulled his safety mask out of his bag to ease the smell and the toxins entering his lungs.

"Probably one of the worst," Jacob agreed, following suit and putting on his mask.

The living room connected directly to the kitchen; a table was the only thing separating the rooms from each other, it was covered in loose newspapers and two old ashtrays, still littered with cigarette butts.

"What's the date say on the papers?" Mason asked taking his camera out of his bag to take pictures of their newest find. He prided himself as a talented photographer who never missed a single good shot.

"1992," Jacob answered flipping through the majority of them.

"Wow, almost 30 years, I wonder if anyone has come in here since then."

"I doubt it," Jacob said judging by the layers of untouched dust.

They walked through the small kitchen; not much had been left there either, the cupboards were made from an old dark wood, cracked and falling off the hinges. The counter; covered in dead bugs, more droppings, and dust. Mason opened one of the cupboards, carefully, but it fell off its hinges completely with a quick but loud thud on the floor.

"Oops sorry," Mason called out.

"I think it's OK, I doubt anyone will notice," Jacob said with a smirk.

Mason continued to snap pictures of everything he could, this house, though small and filthy was one of the most fascinating. It was the feeling he had while being inside of it, not like that typical haunted feeling, but that he shouldn't be there and this would not have been a good place to live.

"Hey Mas, let's go check out the basement," Jacob said loudly, interrupting Mason's thoughts.

"Alright," Mason nodded following behind Jacob.

To the left of the kitchen was a literal square hole in the floor, with a step ladder leading down to the basement. Although the word basement was an overstatement as neither of them had seen one like this before.

The floor was gravel, not wood or concrete, and the gravel was covered in dead rats.

"Sweet Jesus," Mason cried out turning ten shades of green.

Jacob wandered the basement cautiously as to not step on any of the rats, looking for anything that had been left down there. The only things he could see were a washer and dryer, an old-fashioned school desk, and randomly scattered toys.

"Kids lived here?" Jacob wondered out loud.

"Jake, I need out of this basement," Mason shouted before vomiting all over the gravel. The smell down here was rancid, even through their masks it was by far the worst smell he had ever experienced.

It was at that very moment that both of them heard what sounded like footprints on the ceiling.

Mason, now incredibly pale, looked directly at Jacob, who had also turned white. They had never been caught before; would this be the first time?

The footprints stopped for a moment and both men were able to catch their breath.

"Maybe it was just a rat," Jacob suggested looking down at the ground where hundreds of rats had met their fate.

"That couldn't be a rat!" Mason commented,

"They have stopped, lets get out of here before I throw up again," Mason continued.

They climbed the step ladder and before they had reached the top, the footsteps started again, but they walked through the kitchen, and instead of leaving they bravely turned right and down a long hallway.

The first room to the right was the bathroom, the floors were completely torn up, and thick black mold covered the walls. The bathtub; an ugly mustard yellow was full of dirt and what they assumed were pieces of drywall. An old potty chair sat broken next to the toilet, rusted and cold.

The next room was the first bedroom, a single mattress lay on the floor, with pieces of the ceiling lying atop of it. Mason took a few pictures before they moved on, the damage to this room was too extensive to explore further. There were two more doorways, one to the left and one straight ahead, they decided to go left first. As they were about to enter the room they were hit with a blast of cold air, stunned for a moment but continued.

This bedroom had two single beds; both wooden, one to the left of the room and one to the right. There was writing on the walls, broken toys lying along the hard and cracked floor, Mason stepping on an old doll missing an arm.

"Doesn't seem like a place kids would live, does it? Jacob asked looking at all the toys that had been left here.

"Not really," Mason agreed.

The room was full of junk, not just toys but broken dressers, tattered clothing, and other unidentifiable miscellaneous items. Jacob walked over to the closet, having to climb over all the junk, Mason helped him open the closet doors when a small voice called out behind them, "What are you doing?"

They stopped dead in their tracks, almost paralyzed for a moment, but with his heart pounding Jacob turned around and came face to face with a little girl.

She was tiny, with bright green eyes and dark brown hair pulled into a side ponytail.

Mason swore loudly but stood frozen in his place.

"Get out of here, this is not a place you want to be!"

"Jake, is she a ghost?" Mason called out, still not moving from his spot but pinching his arm to make sure he was awake.

"I am not a ghost," the little girl snapped.

"Then what are you?" Jacob asked her kindly.

The girl looked at both men, narrowed her eyes, and said,

"I told you to leave!"

She sat down on the bed to the right, covering her eyes. She had an unkempt appearance, as though she hadn't showered in years, her clothing covered in stains.

"Do you live here?" Mason asked, finally leaving his spot by the closet and approaching the little girl.

She removed her hands from her eyes, "Please leave," she repeated but this time sounded terrified.

"We won't hurt you, little girl, we want to help you," Jacob said trying to comfort her.

"My name is Sam and why do you think you can help?"

"We can try, did you die in this house?" Mason asked.

"I told you I am not a ghost!" She roared loudly.

Sam tried to stand tall, but was still so small, "I am just stuck in this place, I was moved out of here when I was eight years old, but the day we moved I never fully left."

"So, you…"

"I did not die!" she reminded him and continued on,

"This was not a good place to live; it was not a home, just a place to sleep. It was cold, we were hungry and the mice always found me," She shivered.

"Who was hungry?"

"My brother, sister, and I."

Mason and Jacob exchanged looks of disbelief; this couldn't be real, Sam didn't look ghost-like, she was solid, incredibly pale, but very much real looking.

"You really want to know what it was like for us back then?" She asked.

"Yes," they cried in unison wanting to solve this mystery.

Another wall of cold air hit them, thrown into some unknown fog before it calmed and they stepped into the past. They figured out that Sam was the youngest, judging by the sizes of her siblings who were sitting on the couch while Sam played with her toys on the cold hard floor. A mouse ran up beside her causing Sam to scream then jump to the couch sobbing while her brother chased the mouse away.

Before either of them could react, the scene changed to Sam standing in the long hallway close to her bedroom, with her hands over her ears. In the background they could hear yelling and crashing, a man's voice screaming obscenities, which kept getting louder and more intense. After a couple of moments passed Sam ran into her room, opened the closet door, and sat down on the floor inside before sliding the door shut. She cried and hid her eyes, covering her ears to not to hear anymore.

Different scenes flashed before Jacob and Mason's eyes, hard to watch knowing what she lived in, this tiny little girl who shouldn't have been exposed to these conditions.

The last memory she showed them was that of a moving truck, a tall man with dark hair and beard and dark eyes stood on the steps watching the children putting their things inside of the truck. He said nothing, but after a few minutes, he turned and went inside, closing the door harshly behind him.

The fog returned and they were back in the present, "I told you, this is not a place you want to be," Sam whispered.

"I understand now," Jacob said.

Sam looked at him but said nothing.

"So, you're not haunting this house, it's actually the house haunting you!" Mason interjected.

"The house follows you everywhere, even into the future," Jacob finished.

Again, Sam stayed silent except for a few quiet sniffles.

"No one is going to hurt you, Sam you are safe," Jacob assured her.

"I'm never safe."

"Well, there is no one here I promise you, we looked at almost every inch of this home except for the last room."

"That's his room, I never go in there," She told them.

"Why?"

Sam once again narrowed her eyes in a way that said stop asking questions.

"Ok, I'm sorry," Mason said.

"There will always be someone here; I can feel it, I can still smell the cigarettes burning. I can still hear the yelling; the crying and I still feel the fear."

Sam laid down on her old and musty bed making both men cringe.

"What can we do to save you?" Jacob asked her.

"I don't know," she responded coolly.

"What if we tore it down, or set it on fire," Mason asked.

"Dude, we don't ruin houses!" Jacob interrupted angrily.

"What? Do you think anyone would really miss this place?" Mason replied.

They argued back and forth for a moment before Sam interrupted, "You can destroy the house, but I will still live here trapped in my memories."

Jacob and Mason looked at each other not knowing what to say or do.

Sam then walked out of the bedroom and into the hallway, she began pacing back and forth.

"Wait come back," Mason yelled after her.

"You're safe now!" Jacob said.

Sam didn't respond, her weeping now echoing the halls.

The house then faded into darkness....

Sam awoke; covered in a cold sweat, dripping from head to toe. Her green eyes staring at the ceiling, the light from her TV casting a glow around her bedroom. Her heart was pounding, thinking about her old home and the years she spent living there. A single tear rolled down her face which she promptly wiped away along with the sweat that had gathered on her forehead.

"It was just a dream, I'm safe now," Sam reminded herself.

Before going back to sleep Sam went to her daughter's room, where she saw her fast asleep curled up with her stuffed animals.

"I will always keep you safe my baby," Sam whispered before going back to bed. Closing her eyes, she saw her old home once more but watched as it crumbled helplessly to the ground.

As she drifted off to a deeper sleep; she saw a dove walking peacefully on the ground where the house once stood. The little girl walked innocently and happily beside the dove, and as the beautiful bird took off in flight, the girl walked towards the sun, smiling. She was finally free.

MY MIND IS ALL IN MY HEAD

by Shauna Woodbury

The day had begun. Simple. It was early. Maybe 5 am. The sun had frozen its rusty head at that moment just peaking over the sliver of black cloud from last night's darkness. It was simple. Breathe. Begin. He was simple. To breathe and begin wasn't. This endeavor would require movement and initiative. It was early. We know this. Seems simple. One arm, one leg, one eye. Move. Nope not so simple. This will be it. The moment. I will tell him again go. Go now. Simple right?

Hand on the doorknob. One final look around the naked hallway. There were never any pictures up. Only the nicotine-colored walls greet our eyes each day. The orange sunlight just pronounced the discolored teeth stained shade of this hallway. Hand still on the doorknob.

What am I waiting for? This should be simple. Simplicity has become complicated these days. I turn the knob slowly. I hear the deadening empty thud of my emotions. He is awake. How do I tell him I can't have his boot thundering around inside my skull anymore? He dances in my mind, he kicks the walls of my brain and he stomps his anger until the tears fall. He needs to go. Should be simple, right? Goodbye. One word in one second and it should be over. He will leave my thoughts and I'll feel better. I'll be able to think, to speak, and to achieve without his insults, and backward, damaging Johnny Walker wisdom.

Holding my breath I complete the doorknob turn and shove the door open. It's brighter out than my yellow hallway. There are people and movement and then I hear him laughing.

He hisses "Where are you going? Nobody wants to see you. Stay here. Feed me. Tell me you need me"

I freeze. I can feel his foul breath in my head. I look down the street. Children. They laugh. They don't know how a parasite can become comfortable as you play its decaying host. I can't go. He's seething in anger.

"I said stay," he tells me. " Why would anyone want what little you have to offer?"

I close my eyes and whisper back, "Listen to me.   You...." My voice thins and trails. Not so simple. I huff up and try again looking foolish in my doorway knowing people passing can see my dull egg yolk smeared walls and know I'm not somebody anyone would want.

"Listen. You need to go. Find someone else to abuse. I don't want you here. You hurt my thoughts you..." I trailed off again.

"Shut up!" He is angry. I cringe. Maybe today isn't for me.

Two steps back and I'm in the shadows of my mucous-shaded walls. I hang my head and remove my shoes.

I tell him quietly "You don't matter to anyone either. You need to go. I don't need you. I can't have you. I can't ask nicely anymore. Go!"

He laughed. He swore then he lit up a cigarette and sat down telling me I'm foolish and I need him. Without him, I'd be lost. He was kicking the table leg he was sitting at and flicking glowing embers into the unexplored parts of my mind.

Today is the day. I need to do this. I held my head up. I breathed in and I said, "I want you out!"

My thoughts went silent. No movement. No fear. I began to worry. Did he go? Maybe it was simple. I put my shoes on and opened the door again and attempted to venture out.

A feeling of freedom was building. A hope. My inner critic had been evicted. I made him go.

I can believe again. I can be worthy. Without him... I stopped. I'd lost a friend. We spoke every day. His words were harsh and cruel but I wasn't alone. No. Nope. I have to do this. Do this for me. I stepped through my doorway and out into the bright day. Two steps at a time until I was running to my gate. Out and away! I looked back at my house. I'd left my door open. The hallway was shining bright. I smiled. In that house where all the doors stayed closed. The rooms where I kept the voices. Today was simple after all. I had evicted the inner critic.

I left my house door open. I heard all the other doors in my head open and every one steps out into their day without fear. Worth and Value looked great as they joined me outside yet in the hallways of my skull. Challenge and Achievement were bruised and rattled but they staggered to join us. Love and Hope were battle-worn but they believed in me enough to survive. My head was quiet now and the hallways seemed inviting despite the dullness. I walked a few steps and heard him.

"Oh no. Oh crap," I whimpered.

He said coldly, "Not without me. Not ever!" I was paralyzed. No. I buckled at the knees.

"No! It's simple." I was trying to rationalize with the irrational. "You're gone and I can be hopeful of stability and function; to be capable and proud."

I looked at the ground. Fear was waking up. I forgot to close his kennel. Everyone in the carousel of the psychosis in my mind froze. He was back! No. Simple. He goes. We said goodbye right!

There were whispers. Were they in my head or on the street? I was aware I was being watched. Dignity; it was a small being in my head. It was usually quiet and meek but today I needed dignity to be strong. Rise my child, rise! I fought to not burst into screams hoping Dignity would hear me. Determination suddenly arrived with Focus in a cab. They had been in prison for years. We all together screamed. "Go!"

I heard a door slam. I looked back at my house. It was dark. The windows boarded up and the grass black. Again we had hope. Again we had inner peace. Today wasn't simple. Today was another day. Today he left. Today I smiled. Today I felt hopeful I can carry on.

Across the street, a man walking a dog I couldn't see said, "Hey, why bother? Nobody cares."

Today I had been hopeful. It wasn't supposed to go like this!

I ran down the urine colored hall to my safe place. I recoiled. I almost made it to see the sunrise!

Then I heard him, he was back as my tears fell.

I walked to the bathroom and with my hand on the medicine cabinet, I opened the door and took out the razor blade. I've had enough. The walls were spinning on a black and white spiral.

I heard him stride across the ceramic floor of my minds core. His cowboy boots spanking the hard floor with determination. I pressed the blade to my wrist. He stared through me with his red and black eyes.

One finger at a time he took off his white gloves and tossed them to the floor. Today was supposed to be simple. I was going to be free. He took another forceful step forward almost knocking me over. Then as I pierced my skin and he uttered one word that made me shiver; made me want to battle to rally.

I felt so defeated yet I was still here and he felt it. Again he said the one word and it made my head rattle, "CHECKMATE!"

PERISHING YET PREVAILING

by Tabassum H

I stared hard at the stack of bricks and concrete that stood exorbitantly in front of me. They said this was where life and death stood across one another every day, every minute. They said this was where all your hopes and dreams were either fulfilled or brutally destroyed. But they never said that this was where you would get countless moments of short-lived bliss, or a lifetime of grief.

The automated transparent door opened, as I walked through the whitewashed corridors. I shouldn't have known every nook of those long corridors by heart but I did, like the back of my palm. A familiar face met my gaze with a warm smile blooming on her wrinkled face, as I whizzed past her towards the stairs. I drummed the tips of my fingers along the frigid banister while my mind dwelled on the memories that we once made outside of this building.

It wasn't the first time I trod these stairs, nor was it going to be the last time, yet the same fervency gripped my insides. With each step of mine, the same claws of anticipation curled around my throat. With every second that passed by, I could hear the thumping of my heart against my ribs. With every breath that I held back, those flutters were enlivening in the pits of my stomach. And, as I got nearer to that familiar room, my eyes stung and burned just like the day when I had first set my foot in there. And just like that, everything felt unfamiliar and impeccably surreal.

I twisted the doorknob, lingering my hold on it as I let the coldness of its metal pierce through my palm. Letting out those held back puffs of air, I opened the door – only to stumble back as the appalling stench of antiseptic hit me hard, splashing a fleeting snippet of the reality that laid still ahead of me.

"Good morning!" – I chirped, walking to the nearby couch and plopping my bag onto it with a soft thud.

I could feel the familiar sense of anticipation seeping back into me; twisting the knots tightly in the pit of my stomach, causing my heart to beat at an erratic pace, as I waited for you to greet me back; as I waited for your arms to go behind me and hold me firmly; as I expected you to plant a soft kiss at the top of my head like you did every morning that we had woke up to with our souls entangled and resounding giggles.

I turned around, expecting you to be waiting with your arms open to embrace me, but there you laid on the white bleached bed; instead of taking me into those arms of yours, there you were laying on that bed with your arms hooked to those large machines that kept beeping away in the background. Instead of wishing me a good morning, there you were sleeping with the oxygen mask at the top of your mouth that helped you to breathe and push air into those collapsed lungs of yours. Instead of engulfing me into the web of your warmth, there you laid static like a statue, absolutely stoic and impassive.

I shook my head, attempting to erase that pang of disappointment that now clouded all of my anticipations. I broke my gaze from your direction, trying to soothe the pang of ache that had now taken over my heart. Perhaps, it was a curse to expect anything now, but that wouldn't stop me from expecting something that my heart yearned for. Perhaps, it was sinful to keep relighting that extinguishing blaze of hope in the depths of my mind, but that wouldn't stop me from hoping for something that my soul needed to be alive.

They said you wouldn't be getting up from that horrible bleached bed. They said you wouldn't be saying anything out of your mouth anymore. They said you wouldn't be opening your lids any moment from now. They say you were letting go of the will to fight and survive with every passing second. But, whatever they said couldn't stop me from loving you; whatever they threw at my face couldn't refrain me from loving what my heart beats for; whatever they uttered with a label of truth along with it, couldn't make me stop from fighting this unwanted battle with you.

I slouched down on the couch, bringing my bag into my lap. My fingers grazed along the shriveled and crinkled letter as I took it out of the bag. I traced the faint outline of my name that you had drawn at the top left corner of it with dark black ink. It's been a year and eight months to be exact since the day you left this piece of paper at the doorstep; just the night before my birthday – the birthday that we were supposed to spend together, but never got to do so.

A bitter laugh escaped my mouth, as I saw the words that the letter retained perfectly even after so many days. I could find my lips forming a curve as my eyes took in the words that rested on the paper for the hundredth time. It promised an imperishable forever, not this perpetual waiting and longing. It held the vows of love and an abiding companionship, not this relentless yearning to get my share of love back.

The similar feeling of trepidation sank into the empty depths of my soul again, as I waited to hear your footsteps to approach me sneakily; as I waited for you to walk towards me, snatching the letter from my hands and tearing it into several shreds; I anticipated your hands to hold mine and drag me out of this dread-filled place called a hospital to create the world that we had dreamt to weave and adorn together. I expected you to wrap your arms around my stiff shoulders, telling me that you were perfectly alright and always mine.

I lifted up my gaze, with a salient hope gnawing at my insides; But all I got was the amplifying silence, a silence that overshadowed every ounce of hope that ever grew in the back of my mind. All I saw, was the unkempt rise and fall of your chest as you laid there with the ventilator wheezing beside your unbudging body. All I heard, was the ear-splitting laughter of the white painted walls of the room, mocking at my futile will to wait until those eyes of yours open.

I let out a heavy sigh, letting the fading hope out of my soul as I tried to stop the cracks of my heart from resurfacing, only to wail and ache against my ribs. I walked to your medicine cart, sorting out the medicines that were messily scattered. I removed the used bottles of medicines, disposing of them in the trashcan when the sudden creak of the door opening behind me caused me to jump slightly. The bottle slipped out of my hands, falling into the can with an echoing plump.

And there it was again, the trepidation tugging at my heart once again as I longed to hear your laughter rumbling across the room upon seeing me getting scared; the same anticipation back, nagging me as I craved to listen to your deep chuckles upon seeing the startled look on my face. But I never go to hear that soothing voice of yours, all I heard was the clicking of the nurse's shoe on the white floor as she walked towards you with the tray of medicines and injections. I could feel myself wincing, as the needle pierced through your skin providing you with the aids that you needed to live while you remained immobile and motionless.

I sat on the windowsill, looking back at the sky as it stared at me with its vibrant hues of orange and yellow. I hoped for its hues to fill this blank canvas of my life, just like I kept hoping for you to come and stand across me with two warm mugs of coffee in your hands like you always did during those bleak evenings of winter that we had spent in the arms of one another; I hoped for the sky to fill me in with the vivid colors that my soul once used to wear, just like the way my soul ached for you to get out of that bed and reach out to me; just like my heart still beats with your name entrenched on every tendon of it, whereas your heart kept sinking with every passing day.

Closing my eyes, I inhaled the antiseptic air of the hospital as my mind played back the memories of that catastrophic day behind my shut lids. I wished, you hadn't planned that surprise for my birthday; I wished you hadn't rushed to me that day to pick me up. I wished you hadn't let that car get out of your control that day;

I wished you hadn't stayed back inside the car rather had jumped out of it that day as it fell into the ditch. I wished, I never had received that damned call that broke the news of your disastrous accident to me.

But now, all I ever wished was to see you living the perfect life that you had planned for yourself with me being a part of it. All I wished now, was to see you live without those tubes and wires plugged into your body and those machines constantly beeping around you every day and night. All I wished now, was to see you alive and continue to live with your own will and not with this life support system clinging to you.

I opened your favorite classic while sipping the tasteless cup of tea that I got from the canteen of the hospital. Somehow, I found myself getting used to this nasty tea just like you were to lay on that bed reeking of nothing but bleach and antiseptic. I read aloud another chapter of the book aware that my voice might reach your ears, and perhaps even for a fraction of second, you would just get up because of my ceaseless blabbering. I sat on the wooden stool beside your gurney, as I placed my hand at the top of your cold one – flinching when the usual warmth of it didn't reach me anymore. I brushed the dangling hairs away from your face, as the familiar fragrance of yours struck me.

"Get up, my love.." I mumbled, holding your hands to my forehead, and just for a fleeting moment, apprehension was back right at the very core of my soul as I wondered what if your fingers curled around mine any moment from now; what if you leaned your forehead onto mine after I let go of your hands; what if your arms came around me this time, pulling me closer to you and imparting the lost warmth of your love back in every fiber of my existence; But there wasn't any movement, any sound or any response from you except the incessant beeping of the machines surrounding you.

The sudden jerk of my head brought me out of my short nap. I glanced at my wristwatch, it was past ten – it was time for me to go as the visiting hours would come to an end. I walked to the cupboard, getting a comforter out of it, and draped it over you. They said the summers or the winters wouldn't make any difference to you anymore, but I always knew how you couldn't sleep without a quilt resting at the top of you even if it was the hottest or the coldest hour of the season.

I placed a soft peck on your forehead, this time not waiting for your arms to drape around me; this time not expecting you to engulf me in your embrace; this time not silently wishing to hear a good night from your mouth; this time not anticipating you to get up and tell me that you still loved me and that everything would be soon alright. I slung my bag over my shoulder when something flicked behind me – perhaps you just moved your finger, the one that had the silver wedding band residing at the top of it. And just like that, I could feel myself riding a wave of momentary happiness, as hope rekindled itself once again in the depths of my hollow soul.

And just like that, I knew you would get up soon. They said such abrupt movements were my figment of imagination, were just a way of deluding myself away from the daunting reality of us. But my love, I knew, it was your will to live, to fight, and to survive one day to come back to me and leading me towards the life and dreams that we have sewn together.

"See you tomorrow," I whispered, shutting the door behind me as I padded down the stairs, drumming my fingertips along the cold banister before treading past those whitewashed walls of the hospital, only to walk through them again tomorrow with trepidation and flames of hope tugging at the cracks of my heart constantly reminding me that one day this perishing love of ours would certainly prevail over every odd of the world.

IT IS TIME

by T.H. Smart

Sofia Canham woke before her alarm clock with a steely determination. She practically jumped out of bed, catching Phil unaware. He smiled through half-closed eyes and playfully tapped the mattress, coaxing her back to bed.

She laughed, shaking her head, and quickly saying "Not today – today is the big day." She leaned over to give him a kiss and apologized for waking him.

"Good luck Babe," he said. "Not that you need it. You've got this" he added before rolling over and closing his eyes.

He was soon breathing deeply once again. It amazed her how quickly he could fall asleep. She would lie awake for what would seem like hours listening to his soft deep breathing, and its soft, rhythmic sound would gently invite her to fall asleep. But this morning, she had places to be – or rather just one very important place to be.

Late Friday afternoon, she received a text message from her boss, James Wood, requesting a 9 am meeting at the office on Monday morning. He had ended the message with the words, 'It's good news', and the customary smiley emoticon.

He knew her well. They had built a great working relationship since she joined the division two years ago. James had shown himself to be an approachable and encouraging leader. Over the last two years, she had worked hard, taking on new projects and additional responsibilities to prove that she still had more to give. She knew he appreciated the unique strengths she brought to the team, but the glass ceiling was firmly set in place at P4M Industries. As much as she had progressed in 10 years, she had watched others rise and fall, leave and return, and be welcomed back into the inner sanctum ahead of her, too many times to mention.

A sigh escaped as her thoughts turned to more turbulent times.

Before transferring to Research and Development, she had worked herself to the point of absolute exhaustion. It was never enough for Tony Lake; whose ambition and ego clouded his own judgement as much as his golden words clouded the Board's vision. He could do no wrong, even though his division was failing, and he was shedding team members like a deciduous tree in Autumn, in gale-force wind. What puzzled her the most was his uncanny ability to turn calamity into his own success. She had tried to raise her concerns and suggest better ways of working, but it fell on deaf ears. It seemed that the Board was aware of his lack of track record in management, but they felt he was still the best candidate for the job. It was painfully clear that her own track record and alignment to the corporate way of being meant very little.

The vacancy in R&D opened at just the right time and was a good match for her skill set. She knew James from her early years in the organisation and had always respected his way of working. She picked up the phone and dialed his mobile number. Before doing anything rash, she needed to know whether she had a shot at the position. Her enquiry was met enthusiastically. She remembered the day she had the conversation with Tony advising him that she wished to apply for the role. It was company policy. He cut her short and launched into a monologue of all the plans he had and that if she wanted a seat around the boardroom table, she should stick with him. She tuned out, after all, she was not really needed for this exchange.

She shook herself out of her trance and took the final sip of the now cooled coffee. Grabbing her bags and keys, she headed for the door. Two years had gone by quickly and during the last year, she celebrated her 10-year work anniversary. It had not been all roses and the last year had seen the company adopt a survival mindset - partly because of circumstances beyond their control and partly because of ones they had chosen not to control. Cost-cutting measures had been implemented and new strategies were devised to pull the organisation through. She had spent the first half of the year interrogating and refining the product development processes and partnerships and they were now seeing some really promising results both in terms of cost management and speed to execution.

Relieved to be heading to more pleasant conversations, she hummed along with the radio as she drove to the office. Traffic was kind and before long she was at the entrance boom. A quick swipe of her tag and the boom opened. She parked and took the short walk to the office, still humming the chorus from the last song playing. She set up her laptop at her desk, quickly scanning her email inbox for anything that needed her urgent attention. Grabbing her notebook and pen she made a quick list of the things she wanted to tackle as a priority.

A friendly good morning caught her attention and she looked up to see Amy Steel walking towards her. In her official capacity, Amy was the super-efficient office manager. If you needed something, Amy was the go-to girl. If she couldn't get it, it probably didn't exist. More than that, Amy was a dear friend and trusted colleague.

Amy joined P4M Industries a year after Sofia and over the years, they had shared many coffee chats and sought each other out for advice and guidance when an objective but sympathetic voice was needed. They had also learned to read each other's body language, and Sofia could tell something was bothering Amy this morning. "Coffee later?" Sofia inquired

Amy nodded, smiling gratefully, and replied. "That will be great."

As Amy walked back towards her desk to answer the ringing phone, Sofia watched, wondering what could be bothering her friend. She looked at her watch, it was 8:45 am. Her meeting with James was in fifteen minutes. She jotted down some of the ideas that had been brewing since the weekend. She wanted to show James that she was ready and excited to take that next step they had been chatting about recently. She closed her eyes for a moment and focused on her breathing to settle the butterflies which seemed to have woken up and were now desperately searching for a way out. Her phone pinged. Phil had sent a picture of her favourite MCC on ice with the caption "Looking forward to celebrating the good news later".

Putting her phone into her desk drawer, Sofia picked up her notebook and headed down the passage to James's office. As she approached, she could hear James's animated voice within. He sounded upbeat, excited. Figuring he was on the phone, and not wanting to interrupt, she gingerly peeked around the door jam, not wanting to interrupt but wanting to show him she was there.

James beamed and jumped up from his seat. "Come in, come in. I would like you to meet Thandi."

Sofia was not expecting anyone else to be in the office with James and paused as her mind started racing. She did not recall James mentioning Thandi Ndlovu in any of their recent conversations. Thandi stood up and reached out a perfectly manicured hand. Her beautiful face was framed by perfect braids. "Hi, I am so looking forward to working with you," Thandi said. "I've heard so much about you and the improvements you have made in the division. We are going to be able to do great things from the foundation you have built."

Sofia met the extended hand with her own and smiled, hoping that her face was not showing the bewilderment she was suddenly feeling.

Sofia took a breath and as calmly as she could manage, said "I must apologise if I seem a little taken aback. It seems I am a little out of the loop this morning."

She shot a questioning look in James's direction.

His gaze dropped and he gestured to both ladies to take a seat. "Allow me to close the loop", he said. "The Board has been in conversation with Thandi for a little while and just last week, it seems our stars aligned. With Thandi's current contract wrapping up in the next few weeks, she was in the position to accept our offer to head up our Product Development portfolio. As you know, we have an aggressive target to meet and Thandi's experience in Product Ownership and Disruptive Technologies is going to be a real game-changer for us. We are lucky to have her."

Sofia sat, trying to follow the conversation as it bounced between the two of them. Neither of them seemed to notice her silence or her presence.

'This was good news!' she thought to herself as she struggled to contain her emotions. As the conversation lulled, she sat forward in her seat, a feeble smile winning the emotional battle for the time being. "Well, this is certainly a game-changer. If there is nothing else right now, I do need to excuse myself. A to-do list awaits. It was lovely to meet you Thandi," Sofia said as she rose to her feet.

Back at her desk, she sat staring blankly at the screen, trying to process what had just happened. She had been blindsided and the to-do list now seemed pointless. Doubt and anger swirled.

Amy walked up with a concerned look on her face. "I think you might need that coffee a little more than me right now," she said. Sofia blinked back tears, replying "Yeah, let's go. It seems there is nothing I can do here right now."

As Sofia reached for her bag, Amy put her hand on Sofia's forearm and gave a little squeeze. Quietly she said, "They really don't deserve you, you know."

Amy had seen the requisition forms come through that morning and put two and two together. As soon as she saw the look on Sofia's face after the meeting, she knew her worst suspicions had been confirmed.

Sofia texted Phil 'Not the good news I was hoping for. We will have to celebrate another day. Chat later XXX.'

Phil met her at the door as soon as she got home. She fell into his embrace burying her head against his chest and sobbed. It had happened again, and she was reminded how fickle the corporate world was. She felt betrayed and foolish for having believed that this time would be different. She sighed deeply as her tears subsided. Phil lifted her head and kissed her gently on the forehead.

"Go freshen up. Dinner will be ready in a few and there is a cold bottle of MCC that needs opening."

She smiled weakly, gratefully complying with his instruction.

She reemerged fifteen minutes later, dressed in jeans and t-shirt, barefoot and her wet hair brushed back away from her face. Phil handed her a champagne flute, adding with a cheeky smile, "Who said bubbles was only for celebrating? It's also great for drowning sorrows and plotting revenge."

She laughed and took a sip, savouring the crisp brut as it bubbled on her tongue. Sofia narrated the events of the day over dinner, interspersing the narrative with the questions she had wanted to ask all day and momentary rantings of frustration.

Phil listened compassionately, hiding the annoyance he could feel agitating inside. He knew this had meant everything to Sofia. She was perfectly capable and yet continued to be overlooked and exploited. They had said themselves that she had proved her worth, time and time again, but seemed hellbent on withholding the rewards that would prove to her they meant it.

"Why do you still care so much, after all they have done?" he asked.

He had asked that question before. This time she did not answer right away. She sat quietly in her uncertainty. Finally, she looked up at him again, the tears stinging her eyes once more.

"I don't know anymore", she responded sadly.

"Maybe you need to find something else to care about, in addition to me that is," he quipped.

She looked at him and laughed. He was right. She sat back on the couch and settled into the cushions. With one of Phil's action movies playing, her mind was free to explore the idea of finding something else.

Over the next few weeks, Sofia kept a close watch on the existing projects, making sure they were going to plan. When Thandi called, she patiently talked her through the processes and projects to get her up to speed. Her check-ins with James had become more and more transactional. When her attempts to open a conversation about what had transpired were dismissed out of hand, she realized she could no longer trust him. He seemed to be content with the progress being made and the recommendations coming through from Thandi. Sofia determined that was enough and continued to give the best she could during her workweek. It was just a job after all.

She worked well with Thandi. Thandi made it easy for her to still contribute to the strategies and actions for the division and soon they had fallen into a good rhythm. Their strengths complimented each other and Thandi was quick to show her appreciation for Sofia's efforts. It helped to soothe the disappointment Sofia had felt initially. But she had come to terms with the way things were.

They were close to achieving their divisional goals for the financial year. Things were looking up.

During one project close-out, Thandi looked across the table at her, asking permission to change the subject.

"By all means, fire away", Sofia responded, sensing there was a question coming.

"What I have been trying to figure out, Sofia is why you didn't take the job. You have all the qualities, not to mention the experience and knowledge. I think we make a formidable team, but I can't help but wonder," Thandi enquired.

Sofia took a deep breath and looked directly at her, replying "I thought I had, but it was never offered to me."

At that moment, Thandi realized the heartache and disappointment that Sofia had been carrying for months. She sat back in her chair and sipped her coffee. The look on her face suggested she was contemplating how Sofia had continued to show up every day giving her best, even though she had been handed a pretty raw deal.

A few days later, James called Sofia to a meeting. Before heading to his office, Amy came over with a beautiful bouquet of flowers delivered for her. She was just wrapping up a phone call and as she ended the call, Amy couldn't help but notice she was beaming.

"Good news?" Amy asked.

"Yip! Coffee later?" Sofia responded. "Are those for me? They're beautiful."

She breathed in their fragrance. She opened the accompanying card. A small business card fell out onto her desk. Inside the card, were the words: 'It is time. Follow your heart.' She picked up the business card and ran her thumb across the printed job title. CHIEF CREATIVE OFFICER. She tucked the note and business card into her pocket and headed to James's office.

Thandi was there as well. She smiled to herself reflecting on the first time they had met in James's office. This time though, she was the one holding the wildcard. James started by thanking her for the outstanding contribution she had made to ensure the success of the division. As a result, and on Thandi's compelling recommendation, he seemed delighted to inform her that she was being considered for a new role.

Mixed emotions stirred within Sofia as she wondered how many more hoops and job titles it would take.

James and Thandi were both looking at her, waiting for her to respond. She looked between the two of them, breathing in the silence. She reached into her pocket. She could feel the note and business card still there. Her gaze drifted towards the window. James started to fill the silence, "You are, of course, welcome to give it some thought. Nothing has been finalized as yet, and you would need to be involved in the process."

Sofia smiled at him. "Thank you, James, but that won't be necessary. I will always be thankful for the years I have spent at P4M. Years that have prepared me for greater things. I have learnt so much more about myself than I ever would have imagined. And now, a new journey beckons. You will have my full commitment during handover, but the division is certainly in good hands."

She smiled at Thandi. Looking back at James, she added "It would mean the world to me to have your support. It is time and I must follow my heart."

Back at her desk, she took the business card out of her pocket and reached for her phone. She sent a quick message to Phil "It is done. Dinner reservations at 7 pm. XXX".

She looked again at the business card, at her name printed in bold letters above the title.

Sofia Canham
CHIEF CREATIVE OFFICER.

It was time. She had found her something else to care about.

RUNNING WITH LUCK

by T.H. Smart

"Nervous by any chance?" Steve Ray asked, his voice lilting inquisitively.

Sarah smiled nervously and nodded. He reached out his hand, giving hers a squeeze.

"You know, if you don't feel ready, you don't have to go out," he reassured her. "No one is going to question you for not being there tomorrow." He quietly added, "I do wish I could be there with you."

Sarah looked up at him. "I know," she said, "but you have a world to save Dr. Worry-a-lot. And I'll be okay. I'm not going to be alone."

He laughed at her feeble attempt to allay his concerns.

She smiled bravely before adding "I'm good. Really!"

He wanted to believe her, but something still niggled at him. There was sadness in her eyes and earlier in the week she had barely managed to escape another panic attack while out riding. She relayed the story of how one of the crew showed up out of the blue, staving off the attack when an inconsiderate driver had almost sent her crashing into the gutter on a narrow stretch of road. Shaken up she had stopped where she thought it would be safer. Steve was grateful that someone was there to sit with her until she felt strong enough and safe enough to continue.

He knew she was still struggling to sleep, and he couldn't help but worry. He bent down, gently kissing her forehead. "Well then, I'm off. Get some rest tonight and promise me you'll be safe out there tomorrow. Doctor's orders."

She turned her attention back to her race kit spread across the bed, mentally going over everything.

He paused in the doorway, watching her. Her hand rested nostalgically on the custom race kit, proudly displaying their warrior emblem.

At the hospital, Steve looked over the triage list at the cases brought into the ER just before he arrived. He looked up at Helen who was getting the nurse station ready for the night shift.

"What is it about shift change that invites the crazy and stupid out to play?" she asked good-humoredly when she looked up.

Steve laughed. "Indeed," he responded, "well, I best be off to check on STUPID 24 then."

As he headed off to the ward, his thoughts drifted to Sarah. He had wanted to be there in support of her first big race. He wanted to cheer her on from start to end. He was so proud of what she had achieved in so short a time. But the pandemic had been hard on the hospital. The frontline was brutal, and they were all doing what they could to provide the essential care so many needed. One good thing that had come from the pandemic for the medical sector at least, was the curfews and alcohol restrictions. Alcohol-related trauma cases had dropped by almost sixty percent; a small mercy at least. But there was still plenty to be done.

In the ER, Steve regularly saw what happened when the worst of mankind was let loose, through negligence, stupidity, or pure hatred. Innocent bystanders caught in the crossfire of gang disputes; street racers losing control of over-powered vehicles; and the road traffic collisions typically caused by alcohol, speed, or a combination of the two.

As he walked up to Bed 24, he could see the broken body of the young woman on the bed. He looked at her chart, considered the circumstances jotted down, and reclassified her as UNLUCKY 24.

She had been riding pillion when an impatient driver cut across the intersection sending bike, rider, and pillion catapulting over the vehicle. At least they were wearing protective gear. He could hear the rhetoric already: 'She was lucky to have survived.' Her companion had not been so fortunate.

At her bedside, he had one thought in mind, keep her stable! Everything else could wait. One day she would understand that she had been lucky. Steve knew that journey would not be easy. He hoped she would have the support of family and friends to help her to full recovery. As a doctor, Steve knew that medical science could not heal every hurt. He had seen what friendship could do through Sarah's life.

Satisfied that she had everything ready for the next morning, Sarah settled down with a cup of Chamomile tea and the race route map. She considered each of the three stages and calculated her target pace for each to ensure a good finish well before the cut-off time. She picked up a photograph of the crew taken the morning they accepted the Regal Challenge. Sarah fell asleep with the photo of the crew clutched against her chest.

The alarm beeped at 4 am Race Day. Sarah checked her phone. There was a message from Steve. 'Good luck, thinking of you today babe! I'll see you at the finish line. You've got this.'

"No, we got this," she said, speaking to the photograph on the bed.

Sarah dressed, made sure she had every thing, and headed for the door.

On the drive to the Regal Park, her mind wandered back to events that had led her to the crew. She remembered sitting in Doctor Hammond's Oncology Practice reception at Regal General, anxiously waiting for her check-up. For the first time in the two years since her diagnosis, she was starting to feel strength returning. She desperately wanted to be more active and had spoken to Steve about starting up cycling again. He had been supportive but cautious and urged her not to jump into anything too strenuous, too fast. The door opened and Sarah looked up hoping to see Steve. Instead, the frame walking confidently into the room and announcing his arrival, was tall, and tanned with short blonde hair, the brightest blue eyes, and what seemed like the biggest, warmest smile ever. Smiles were in short supply around there. He took the seat across from Sarah.

Steve rushed in, looking a little harassed but relieved to see her. "Hey," he smiled, "I wasn't sure I was going to make it. Traffic through the lobby was crazy," he joked.

Blue Eyes looked up and his big warm smile broke his face again. "Dr. Ray!" He exclaimed, "It's good to see you Doc."

Sarah looked between Steve and Blue Eyes quizzically, grateful for the distraction. The waiting game was pure torture.

"I suspect you don't remember me, what with all the people you legends save in the ER every day, but you fixed me up real good a few months back when I took a nasty tumble off my bicycle."

That was enough to jog Steve's memory.

"How are you doing?" He grinned. "If I recall, you had overshot the corner to the hospital coming in for a check-up and ended up in the cactus bed. You made our day in the ER."

Blue Eyes roared with laughter.

"Yip, what can I say, I had just got my best time on the Boulevard sprint and momentarily forgot I needed to slow down before coming to a stop. I guess I could not have chosen a better place to crash – well, except for those damn spikes. Happy to report I have been working on my stop and I think I have it down. I'm holding thumbs that if all goes well today, Doc Hammond will give me the all-clear to start training for the Regal Classic."

"That's great. My wife Sarah is also hoping for an all-clear to get started with cycling again. Any tips?" Steve asked.

"Just one, do it!" Wes said enthusiastically. "There are a few of us warriors that get together regularly for a ride. You should come and join us sometime. We don't take ourselves too seriously. Just love to get out there in the fresh air and get the legs spinning and blood pumping."

Blue Eyes introduced himself as Wes and handed over a business card.

"And you'd be welcome too Doc," he added. "The way I ride, it's probably best to have a doctor around." He was laughing again.

Doctor Hammond was pleased with Sarah's progress, and putting to rest Steve's doctorly and spousal concerns, endorsed the idea of her starting with some easy cycling.

As the months passed, Sarah got fitter and stronger. To combat the boredom that was fast setting in with the indoor trainer, Steve encouraged her to look out for a club or group of social riders she could join. "Safety in numbers," he always said.

Her Google search returned several pages and multiple links. Amongst the online ads, was a search result about a local sports story. She clicked on the link. As the page opened, she immediately recognized the blue eyes and warm smile of Wes amongst the group. It was a feel-good article that had chronicled the formation of an amateur sports team. Each member of the group had won their battle against dread disease. Having found a new lease on life through cycling and running, the group was hosting an information session for interested members of the public that were keen to get into running, cycling, or both. Sarah bookmarked the page, making a mental note to chat to Steve about it later.

Wes had assembled the most amazing community of warriors. There was something special about them that went beyond the fact that they had overcome ridiculous odds. Sarah felt at home with them from the very first ride. She had been anxious about joining them as she wasn't sure she would be fast enough or fit enough, but it had not been necessary. Their group philosophy was to leave no rider behind. It wasn't long before Sarah found herself going further and faster. She even got up the courage to take up running, working with a coach to guide her.

During one post-run coffee, Wes suggested they sign-up for the Regal Road Challenge – a classic duathlon event comprising a 10km run, 60km cycle, and finally a 10km run. It was 9 months away and with the level of training they were doing, Wes was confident that they would be able to comfortably compete in the popular event. Nothing seemed impossible for Wes and as a result, nothing seemed impossible for their crew.

Sarah enjoyed having a non-medical event to look forward to for a change, and threw herself into training and preparations, even designing a logo and custom kit for them. A chill drew her from her reverie as she was reminded that this race was the one that would be impossible for Wes.

Sarah headed to the demarcated participant parking area. Turning off the car, she rested her head on the steering wheel for a few moments. Eyes closed, she breathed in and out slowly and audibly, attempting to counter her nervousness and keep her emotions in check. Blinking back tears, she got her gear and headed to where the crew had agreed to meet. Jen, Lee, and Mel were already waiting. Mel had arranged coffee and poured Sarah a cup. Lee chimed in excitedly,

"Sarah, you did a stellar job with this kit. It looks awesome!" Jen and Mel nodded.

After a quick selfie, they waited for the call to line up at the start.

Steve looked at his watch. It was 6:30 am. Sarah would be 30 minutes into the first leg of the race. He closed his eyes for a moment uttering a silent prayer. He checked his phone and saw Sarah had sent a selfie of the crew at the starting line. In the background, a blurred figure caught Steve's eye. He assumed it was one of the other athletes, most likely warming up frenetically on the spot oblivious of the selfie they were photobombing. He put his phone back into his pocket. He had done his last rounds and before heading to the Doctors Lounge for a coffee and croissant, he wanted to check in one last time on UNLUCKY 24. She had been transferred to ICU just after midnight. The nurse at the ICU desk smiled up at him.

"Good morning Dr. Ray, and who might you be checking in on today?"

Even though Steve worked in the ER, he was a frequent and well-liked visitor to the ICU. He would always drop by to check on the patients that had come through on his watch.

"Young woman, motorbike accident," Steve listed her injuries.

"Ah, that would be Miss Vicky Steel. She is over in Bed 3. All stable. She was lucky."

There was that word again. Lucky! They had said the same thing to him four months earlier when they brought in three cyclists. Two of them had taken the full force of the car when the drunken driver misjudged the turn. They were in really bad shape. Steve's blood ran cold as he recalled the moment they were wheeled into the ER and he recognized the faces. He didn't always know the names of those that entered, but that day he did. It was Sarah, Wes ,and Mike.

Sarah had been lucky, although she still did not necessarily see it that way.

The memory haunted Steve as much as it did Sarah. She had been devastated that Wes and Mike would miss out on Regal. It made her more determined to compete. As the training helped her keep focused on the goal, rather than the accident, Steve encouraged her at every turn, congratulating her on the good training days and reminding her how far she had come on the not-so-good ones. It had been going well, most of the time. Every now and again, a selfish driver would do something stupid which would trigger a panic attack. She insisted she wanted to carry on. If Wes and Mike could not do it, she wanted to do it for them.

It was the final leg of the race, a 10km run. Just after the 6km marker, Sarah felt the fatigue starting to set in and her focus dipped. Her mind starting racing with a million thoughts. It was running so fast, it could have easily broken the record if it had not needed to be tethered to her physical body to count. That humorous reflection succeeded in bringing her back to the moment. Realising she was running alone, she glanced at her watch. She could feel herself slowing down. The watch face indicated that she was set to achieve her best time. If she could just keep it up and not let her head get the better of her.

Her breathing got shallower and more panicked. She tried focusing on a point in the distance to take her mind off the rising anxiety. It was then that she heard his voice.

"Just 3kms to go." She turned to see Wes running up alongside her.

"What are you doing here?" she gasped.

"You didn't really think anything was going stop me from doing this race did you?" he laughed.

"Your timing!" she exclaimed, shaking her head in disbelief. He always knew when she needed an extra dose of encouragement.

Wes helped her steady her pace the rest of the way. As they rounded the last corner, she could see the finish line ahead. She looked at Wes, and said, "We did it! We really did it!"

Wes smiled. "No Sarah, you did it. You did it for me. Thank you!" And with that, he was gone.

Sarah crossed the finish line alone, exhausted, relieved. Steve was waiting for her as he had promised. Before he could get to her, a race official took her by the arm and guided her across to a nearby table where other race officials were sitting with timers and laptops. Perplexed by the camera flashes and sports journalists asking for comments, she looked back for Steve who was now a couple of steps away. He swept her up in his arms and spun her around.

"Easy Doctor Worry-a-lot", she laughed feebly. "It was just a race."

"No babe, that was not just a race. You just took regional champ in the Women's Senior Division. Didn't you hear it announced as you crossed the finish line?" he asked.

She looked back at the officials who were nodding in agreement. She knew she had got separated from the others but didn't for one minute consider it was because she was leading the pack. She heard someone from the sidelines shout her name. As she looked up in the direction of the voice, she saw Mike applauding from his wheelchair. Behind him stood Wes. She mouthed the words thank you. Their proud smiles could not have been any wider. She looked again at the Race Official explaining something. Her gaze drifted back to the guys, and rested on Mike, still smiling, seated in his wheelchair. Alone.

Steve wrapped his arms around her, whispering into her ear how very proud he was. For the first time in well over four years, Sarah thought of herself as lucky.

OREGON TRAIL

by Vaughn Roste

Sarah was brushing her hair in the mirror, and some came out. A lot. We had to go before it was our teeth.

"You said we would," I reminded her. "You promised."

"Fine." She sighed. We both knew this day would come.

It was a hike that had always been on my bucket list – a rarely-travelled path up the Oregon coast. Apparently, it had gotten even more dangerous in recent years. Emergency services ceased operations six months ago, cell phone service theoretically worked but was spotty – but just who were you going to call for help now anyway? Everyone was on their own. Surround yourself with close friends and admit no one else into your circle.

But this was where I wanted to go. Sarah might have been content to never leave the house again, but it was time – now or never.

We left all the food out for the cat and drove as far as we could. We each had backpacks, but not much in them. We wouldn't need much. I left the car open and the keys on the seat, in case anyone else wanted to use it.

The stench of the dying city was soon behind us. We hiked north along the coast, sometimes high above the surf, sometimes so close we'd get wet in the wind. No sandy beaches here – this coastline is rocks. Water pounds relentlessly against crags and cliffs. It was ironic: both exhilarating and calming at the same time.

We weren't alone on the trail either: an hour in we looked back and saw a young girl – 16, maybe, not so much younger than Sarah – in a red rain jacket standing way too far out on the rocks. We had just passed that spot minutes earlier. Now, there she was, standing too close to the sea.

"Hey!" Sarah yelled at her. I did too: "Get back! It's not safe!" We gestured wildly to try and call her back. I know she heard me because she looked right at me. Then she took a step further, towards the water, in spite. It was the last intentional move she made. I realized this was her decision – and I wasn't going to save her.

The surf crashed, and she was swept under the wave. I hope she died from hitting the rocks the first time. Maybe she drowned. She was easy to spot, red raincoat in the water being bashed up against the rocks. Sarah couldn't watch, though, and buried her head in my chest - but she didn't say anything. We had no tears to spare for strangers. Soon her battered body was pulled out to sea. No one would see her again. I would be fine if I never witnessed another death again.

The trail eventually veered inland. I don't know how to explain it but several of the plants would seemingly glow a thin fuzzy blue aura. There was like this static charge on them – if you touched them, they would shock you. Nature was getting back at us. Can't say we didn't deserve it.

A torrential rainstorm soon exploded in the sky. We set up a make-shift shelter by stretching out a jacket between the trees. We huddled beneath it, close, for warmth. A fire would have been nice, but there was nothing to burn that wasn't wet. We had seen enough of fire lately anyways.

When the rain let up, we got up and walked ourselves dry. The trees opened up into a clearing where the path meandered through – except now we got our first view of the Venus Traps in person. These things were fifteen to twenty feet high! Venus fly-traps are for flies: these plants ate any meat they could reach, including pigs and cows and, it had been proven, humans. The name seemed right, they seemed otherworldly. At least they couldn't move. It might have been the radiation that caused their mutation, I don't know – I save those questions for the scientists, but the few who are left have more pressing issues on their minds.

The path led to the middle of the clearing, where a proud Venus Trap flowered like a queen. A pile of white bones near her base attested that she was well-fed – I wasn't about to get close enough to examine what she was eating. We kept a wide berth, walking around the edge of the clearing, moving slowly, peering into the darkness hoping there weren't more lurking in the forest. That was not the way we wanted to die. The queen in the middle followed our move as if we were the sun.

Finally, a welcome sight – a cabin, made of wood, smoke curling from the chimney. Two rocking chairs on the front porch offered an irresistible invitation. We approached, almost running. I knocked on the door. "Hello?" I called. "Hello?"

Motion from inside – footsteps – and an old man opened the door: white hair, stubbly beard, crinkly skin. "Welcome!" he said. "We don't get many visitors 'round these parts. Come in, come in... didja get caught in that storm? By the looks of it ya shore did!"

We entered, grateful. "Nice place," I said, admiring the surroundings. It was rustic yet comfortable. "You live out here?"

"Shore do." He smiled with his eyes. "Here, lemme put on the kettle. Take a load off, make yourselves at home." He seemed genuine enough.

"How long you been out here?" I asked. Did the Venus Traps eat bears, I wondered? Moose? Can an apex predator be stationary?

"Figure ten years now at least. Bought the place before the world went to shit, never thought I would actually live out here. But it seems being a hermit is a good thing in a pandemic. Whoda thunk?"

Tobacco stains marred his smile. The tea kettle whistled. When he took it off the fire, I heard bleating out back.

"You raise your own food, then?" I inquired.

"Shore do. Got a trip of goats out back."

"A trip?" I asked.

"Apparently, that's what they're called," he said, not unkindly. "Here's your tea," he offered, stirring in bags from a tin canister. "Do ya want sugar? Sorry, I'm out of honey."

"Everyone's been out of honey since the bees died," I allowed. "Wasn't that the start of it all?"

"Doesn't matter now, does it?" he said. "World's gone to pot last I checked. It's every man for himself. And woman," he added, a concession to Sarah.

"No, you're right," I admitted. "It's survival of the fittest out there."

"Not necessary the fittest," I heard him mutter under his breath.

"Thank you for your hospitality," she said, sipping her mug. "This is delicious."

"Indeed," I said, basically lying. I couldn't place the flavor precisely, but I never drank a lot of tea anyways. It was warm, I didn't care. We ran out of sugar long ago.

"How do you stay safe out here with all those Venus Traps around?" I asked. "We saw a massive one in a clearing not far from – "

"Ah, my garden." He grinned. "If she's fed she won't eat me," he said. "I bring something for her each time I pass. An offering to the gods." He stared at me, waiting.

"This is so nice of you," I said, suddenly really drowsy. "I feel like you can't trust anyone anymore."

Sarah's teacup suddenly clattered to the floor, and her arm went limp in the chair. She was out. She looked so peaceful, just like when I would rock her to sleep in my arms.

"Nope," he admitted gravely. "Ya shore can't."

ABOUT THE AUTHORS

C.N. GREER

Growing up in the Pacific Northwest, C.N. Greer has never been lacking in inspiration. In the last twenty years, she has taken that inspiration and expressed it for the world through the written word. An avid book reader, C.N. Greer is a fantasy writer and a poet. She hopes to share that love of fiction with her daughter. When she's not writing, she's spending time with her family and wrangling the fur babies that keep her life interesting. She believes in the human spirit and a person's capacity for strength and resilience, but she also knows those virtues can be hard won. She is an advocate for equality and compassion, and she hopes to bring some light into this world with her work of poetry and prose. Follow her on Facebook at facebook.com/cngreerpoetry/ and @cngreerpoetry on Instagram

JENNIFER ANDERSON

Jennifer writes from the heart and puts into words feelings and thoughts that others are often not able to. She has great insight into life and people thanks to her strong sense of intuition. She loves putting her pen to paper (yes she is old school) and seeing what comes...she is often as surprised as everyone else by the result. Writing is her church, it's how she makes sense of the world around her, and often finds her words in the, betwixt, that special place between here and there and not really anywhere. Follow Jennifer at: facebook.com/juxtaposedjenn

JENNIFER JENNINGS DAVES

A relative newcomer, Jennifer Daves is finding her place in the world of social media writers. However, she is not limiting her capabilities and is working to stretch her talents to the farthest reaches. Jennifer's writing is as often playful as it is brutal. Two sides of a completely complex and beautiful soul - one that invites you into the garden for tea but warns you of the dangers of sitting too close to the rose bushes, as she plucks the bloody thorns from her heart, one by one, and offers them to you. Whether it is prose, poetry or a song, she will definitely capture your attention as she serves up delicate pieces of her soul. Visit her website iworeabraforthis.com

NICOLE LABONTE

Nicole Labonte is a single mom to one daughter, and a 15 year old cat. She lives in a small city in Ontario Canada. She is a poet, but loves writing short stories and in August of 2020 she self published her first novel, the first of a trilogy, a modern-day fantasy fiction novel titled "The Wand." Nicole loves music; mostly of the post hardcore genre, enjoys playing piano and a lover of live (rock) music. Nicole is a dedicated mom, and a loyal aunt, sister and friend. She has many nieces and nephews that are loved as her own children, and friends who are loved as family. Nicole works full time in the cosmetic industry, and uses her off time to write as much as possible. She started writing at ten years old, and has only continued to find her passion through writing what is in her soul. Follow her on Facebook at facebook.com/nicolelabontewriter

LYSSA DAMON

Lyssa Damon lives in Cape Town, South Africa, in the heart of the winelands with her family and assortment of weird and wonderful pets. Lyssa has written in some form or another since she can remember, starting with a poem about kittens losing mittens in a puddle. She writes poetry, short stories, flash fiction and has recently started work on a novel and hopes to recreate some of her stories as screenplays. Lyssa loves the ocean, talks to moon, and believes in magick. She loves animals and some people. Her ultimate dream would be to own a castle, with an enormous library where she can live, dream, and write full time. Follow her at facebook.com/linesbylyssa and @linesbylyssa on Instagram

KELLI J GAVIN

Kelli J Gavin of Carver, Minnesota is a Writer, Editor, Blogger and Professional Organizer. Her work can be found with Clarendon House Publishing, Sweetycat Press, The Ugly Writers, Sweatpants & Coffee, Zombie Pirates Publishing, Setu, Cut 19, Passionate Chic, Otherwise Engaged, Flora Fiction, Love What Matters, Printed Words and Southwest Media among others. Kelli's first two books were released in 2019 ("I Regret Nothing- A Collection of Poetry and Prose" and "My Name is Zach- A Teenage Perspective on Autism"). She has also co-authored 18 anthology books. With two more books to be released in 2021, she is also working on a large collection of fiction short stories. Her blog can be found at kellijgavin.blogspot.com & @KelliJGavin on Twitter, Instagram and Facebook

VAUGHN ROSTE

Vaughn Roste has written books, plays, poems, peer-reviewed articles, book reviews, program notes for CD liners and Carnegie Hall, and a doctoral dissertation, most of which never paid. His book, The Xenophobe's Guide to the Canadians, published by Oval Books in England (1st edition 2003 through the 8th edition, revised, 2016) just went out of print. Follow him on Twitter @Vaughn09187022

WIL R.P. MCCARTHY

Wil was born in Upstate NY. After his father reenlisted, he moved up and down the East Coast (USA). Never feeling like he belonged. He has suffered from Manic Depression since his brother's death when he was twelve and developed Schizophrenia in his early twenties. His writing is dark at times and will revolve around his problems. It started as a coping mechanism to deal with his issues and has evolved into a want to help others. He wants others to understand they are not alone. Visit his website thestoriesofaravingmadman.wordpress.com and follow him on Facebook at facebook.com/theravingsofamadman

CA NEWRY

Cecil Newry is a Bahamian storyteller and socio-political blogger and provocateur. He has published two books of poetry and is in the midst of publishing a third, along with a book of short stories. Cecil lives in Nassau, The Bahamas.

EMMA GLEDHILL

I feel as though a love of words, stories and books have been a part of me all my life. Books have always been a sanctuary. She tends to lean towards a more melancholy subject matter. She began to write as an adult, after the end of a marriage that she felt she had to escape from rather than end. Writing, mostly indirectly, about the experience and the person she has become since, became a cathartic exercise. Coupling that with finding the man that is the other half to her soul gave her a well of emotion and perspective Emma often draws upon. Being a happily married mother of two small children doesn't always allow her the time to write as she wishes but she wouldn't change that. However it is why it means so much to her to have been chosen to participate in this anthology. Follow her on Facebook at facebook.com/pentopaperc2g

CHARLENE ANN BENOIT

Charlene Ann Benoit, a native of Newfoundland, Canada, began writing poetry at the age of ten. In 2004, she finished her first collection of poems, entitled, Pieces of My Soul. In 2005, she completed her first novel, When Walls Come Crashing Down. Since that time, she has compiled five other books of poetry: In Memory Of (2005), Shattered (2008), Between the Lines (2019), In the Hearts of Gods, Monsters, and Men (2020) and Blood, Tears and Coffee Rings (2020). She has also written a children's book, The Littlest Prince (2015), that is currently on hold for illustrations. She released a short fictional memoir called Death's Daughter in 2020. The Skeptic, her second completed novel, is expected to be released early in the new year. Follow her on Facebook at facebook.com/charleneannbenoit

TABASSUM H

Tabassum Hasnat, a freelance writer of shortform fictitious genres. She sought far and wide in the search of something, that held her heart in passion, and thrilled her psyche ceaselessly. And that something was writing, and losing herself in those tedious tomes of law and literature. Soon, she was blessed to have the recognition of a published writer. She has completed her International Ordinary Levels in science under Pearson Edexcel, and is currently completing her Pearson Edexcel International Advanced Levels, along with law and legal studies. She has her own personal blog on the global platform of Storymirror Pvt Ltd. She has co authored in multiple international anthologies and book compilations, where her writeups have been published on platforms like Amazon, Kindle, Google books, Kobo, Barnes & Noble, and Notion Press. She is aiming to seek a wonderful opportunity to enhance & apply her writing skills in a dynamic workplace. Follow her on Facebook at facebook.com/tabassum.hasnat.10 and @_tashaa8055_ on Instagram

JAY LONG

Jay Long is a New York based author, poet, and natural storyteller. His creative voice can be heard throughout social media and online writing communities. Through his writing and work with other writers, he continues to establish himself as one of today's prolific voices. To learn more about Jay visit jaylongwrites.com or you can follow him on Facebook at facebook.com/writerjaylong and @writerjaylong on Instagram

JANA BEGOVIC

As far back as she can remember, Jana has been fascinated by storytelling. Her love of reading and writing propelled her toward studies of languages and literature resulting in several academic degrees. Among her publications are academic and other articles, the novel "Poisonous Whispers" published by Roane Publishing, poetry, short fiction, art reviews and blog posts featured in literary journals, such as Ariel Chart, Chantwood, the Pangolin Revie, Abstract, Canada Fashion Magazine, and The Black Shamrock. One of her stories was published in the award-winning anthology, The Thin Places, published by Broken Keys Publishing. She is also senior editor/writer of Ariel Chart literary journal and Canada Fashion Magazine. She has been nominated for the 2019 Best of the Net Nominations and the PushCart awards. She lives in Ottawa, Ontario and works for the Government of Canada as an education specialist in the field of military language training. She can be contacted via her Author Page at facebook.com/J.Damselfly/

KATHLEEN LONG

Kathy is a retired RN spending 48 dedicated years with the same hospital serving the community until she retired in late 2015. During her nursing career she received many accolades including the 1984 Humanitarian Award. Kathy is a 2x cancer survivor, mother, grandmother, and proud fur baby owner.

T H SMART

T H Smart is a writer, poet, visual storyteller, and all-round creative spirit. Both creative and strategic, she is as comfortable in the boardroom and training room, as she is in her home studio creating visual and written art. She weaves the threads of inspiration she collects in life and work through her writing. By sharing the beautiful messages that skewer her heart, she hopes to stir up others in love so they might be strengthened and inspired to run after the plans and purposes for their lives. She shares her suburban home in Cape Town, South Africa with her husband, daughter, and four furry friends. You can find more of her writing on her website Warrior for Worthiness (warriorforworthiness.co.za), Facebook (facebook.com/smartmuser), Instagram (tarynhaynessmart) or LinkedIn.

BRANDY LANE

Brandy is making a splash in the poetry world with the recent release of her new book "Where Beautiful Loves"(which is available on Amazon) and has been published in nearly a dozen anthologies within the past several months. She has become known in the Instagram world on several platforms for her passionate way of reading and interpreting poetry. She is working on her second book of poetry, and has big plans for the future, having started her own publishing LLC, Where Beautiful Inks. You can find Brandy on social media at the following: facebook.com/wherebeautifullives/ instagram.com/wherebeautifullives/

JAMIE SANTOMASSO

Jamie is an author from Kansas City, Mo. A writer since the age of five, she has used the literary arts as a means to express her thoughts and feelings through the written word. Jamie takes inspiration from both life experience and imagination to create vivid pictures of love, heartbreak, fantasy, darkness, and other residual works. Her works have received praise for their ability to evoke emotion, paint pictures, and tell stories that the reader can fully immerse and lose themselves in. Follow her on Facebook at facebook.com/spiritofthesonneteer

SAM PALMER

Sam started her love of writing when she won a writing contest in the 4th grade with her essay "How The Lion Got His Name". Since then her writing has evolved over time into darker themes, exploring the grittiest parts of life and human nature. Her passion is creating, whether that's writing short stories, drawing or painting. She went to high school in Las Vegas, Nevada; but now lives in Southern California with her fiance and their two corgis. She spends her free time cooking, traveling, writing, and doing art. Learn more on her blog site. sampalmerstories.com

SHAUNA WOODBURY

Shauna was born in Calgary Alberta Canada. She writes, plays baseball, loves beer and festivals. She writes from a darker side but loves the rainbow fireworks the little happy moments in life bring. She has two sons and a beautiful life partner to complete her world. Her future endeavours hope to include more writing, more living and brighter connections. At the age of 50 her life and literary creations are just beginning. Join her on her journey. Follow her on Facebook at facebook.com/SexLeatherHearts

AMANDA MULLER

Amanda is a college student who graduated from SUNY Adirondack and plans to further her studies to immerse herself into the medical field. At ACC, she played on the college softball team for two years and graduated Cum Laude. Before college, she was homeschooled her whole life along with her four other siblings by her mother. Amanda decided to graduate high school early and completed 11th and 12th grade in her junior year. During that year, she volunteered at Moreau Emergency Squad where she was able to ride along as an observer. She found her passion for writing in high school by reading numerous post-apocalyptic novels. This led her to be curious about how one comes about to write such page turning stories, and became her inspiration to create "MirroRed". You can find her on social media at: instagram.com/amandee_57 & facebook.com/mandy.ashley.77

ABOUT 300 SOUTH MEDIA GROUP

Everyone has a story to tell. And with so many writers choosing to self publish, it is no surprise there are companies and individuals looking to exploit the dreams of those who hope to see their story in print. 300 South was founded by writers in order to help indie authors safely navigate the ins and outs of the self-publishing process.

300 South is not a vanity press. We will never charge you to publish your book because our services are meant to guide, teach, and collaborate with those interested in assisted self-publishing.

Whether you write fiction, nonfiction, or poetry, 300 South can provide active, one-on-one services as you prepare your project for publication. Choosing 300 South will ensure your dreams remain intact and no one benefits from your story but you.

At 300 South, our company's heart and soul are the authors we empower on a daily basis. We constantly strive to serve you the best we can and treat each project as if it's our own. We understand that the end result is not simply words on a page, but an extension of you.

For more information visit our website 300SMG.com and follow us on Facebook at facebook.com/300SouthPublishing

Website: 300SMG.COM
Facebook: FACEBOOK.COM/300SOUTHPUBLISHING
Instagram: INSTAGRAM.COM/300SOUTHPUBLISHING

www.ingramcontent.com/pod-product-compliance
Lightning Source LLC
Chambersburg PA
CBHW021656110726
47902CB00007B/1958

* 9 7 8 0 9 9 7 0 3 5 6 4 3 *